DUST AND INHERITANCE
THE SPYKER RANCH
BOOK ONE

KIRK VOCLAIN

Copyright © 2025 by Kirk Voclain

All rights reserved.

No part of this book may be reproduced in any form or by any electronic or mechanical means, including information storage and retrieval systems, without written permission from the author, except for the use of brief quotations in a book review.

Please review on Amazon and Goodreads. For more info go to my website https://kirkvoclain.com

This is a work of fiction. Names, characters, places, and events are either products of the author's imagination or used in a fictitious way. Any resemblance to real people, places, or situations is purely coincidence.

Still, if you know my good friends Bob and Lisa, and their family, then. you know what inspired this book.

❦ Formatted with Vellum

To my wife, Tammy Voclain.

You were my first reader, my preliminary editor, and my sounding board through every draft, every doubt, and every late night "does this even work?" moment. You never told me what to do, you suggested, and somehow your suggestions always landed right where the story needed to go. Your patience, sharp notes, and steady belief carried this book from first spark to final period.

This one, like all of them, is for you, "My Tammy!"

And to Bob and Lisa Spyker, our vacation friends who turned into something like family.

I can't count how many text messages and calls went back and forth, but I can count the moments that mattered. When I shared my love of writing, you challenged me to write Boots and Stilettos, a clean and wholesome western romance, and that challenge changed everything. Then, in the middle of one of those conversations, one word showed up and refused to leave.

Clem.

You told me the name of Bob's grandfather, and that single name opened a door I didn't know I needed to walk through. Thank you for the spark, the encouragement, and the push that got me moving.

CONTENTS

A Note From The Author	vii
Prologue	1
1. Chapter One *The Arrival*	3
2. Chapter Two *Town, Eyes, and Quiet Measuring*	19
3. Chapter Three *The Fence Line*	30
4. Chapter Four *No Trespassing*	39
5. Chapter Five *The Witnesses*	53
6. Chapter Six *Man and Wife*	62
7. Chapter Seven *Near the Ridge*	79
8. Chapter Eight *The Empty Room*	94
9. Chapter Nine *The Sure Thing*	105
10. Chapter Ten *The Ranch House*	115
11. Chapter Eleven *Debt Settled in Full*	126
12. Chapter Twelve *Goodbye Work*	136
13. Chapter Thirteen *Debt Doesn't Die*	144
14. Chapter Fourteen *Buckle and Bloodline*	151
15. Chapter Fifteen *The Spyker Ranch Is His Now*	161
16. Chapter Sixteen *A Promise On The Ridge*	168
Epilogue	175

The Inspiration	183
About the Author	185
Also by Kirk Voclain	187

BOOTS AND STILETTOS

Prologue	191
1. Chapter One	193
Big Sky Collision	

A NOTE FROM THE AUTHOR

If you found this book during a promotion, thank you for taking a chance on my work.

If you enjoy *Dust and Inheritance*, I'd truly appreciate an honest review on Amazon or Goodreads, or both. Even a few words can help other readers decide if this story is right for them.

You can find more about my books at **KirkVoclain.com**, and you're welcome to join my newsletter for updates on new stories, bonus content, and future promotions.

PROLOGUE

THE BUS TICKET

She almost didn't get on the bus.

The ticket sat on the seat beside her like it belonged to someone braver. Millie checked her watch. 7:17 a.m. Saturday, August 31, 1957. Thirty minutes before departure, in a depot that smelled like stale coffee and old leather.

It was a one-way ticket from Ohio to Montana that promised sixty-seven hours on the road, two cheap hotel stays, and over two thousand miles of thinking time.

Montana.

An entire state that sounded like dust, cattle, and men who didn't smile unless they meant it.

Mildred Caldwell. Millie to the handful of people who still had permission to call her that. She stared at the ticket and tried to make sense of herself. What was she doing? This wasn't a vacation. It wasn't a business trip. It wasn't even a clean obligation.

It was a borderline favor.

Her uncle's last plea kept looping in her head. Again. And again.

Don't let it vanish.

She told herself it was about him. About paperwork and land

and doing the right thing. But the truth sat closer to her ribs than she liked.

She'd bought the ticket herself.

Nobody forced her. Nobody begged her, not in person. She could've stayed home and let the world handle its own mess. She could've folded his letter, put it in a drawer, and let it go quiet.

But Millie didn't fold easily.

The bus rolled into the depot with a hiss and a tired shudder. Doors opened. People moved. The whole place shifted like it had decided time was leaving with or without her.

Millie took a breath, smoothed her dress, and grabbed her suitcase. She took two steps, then stopped.

She turned back. Picked up the ticket. Held it between her fingers like it might burn.

Then she walked straight toward the bus, chin up, shoulders squared, stubbornness leading the way.

She didn't know the man waiting in Montana was a liar, or that she was about to fall for a place that didn't care who she was. She stepped onto the bus anyway.

CHAPTER ONE

THE ARRIVAL

Clem leaned against the fender of his red truck, watching the dust settle at the edge of town. Beside him, Wade spat into the dirt, not bothering to look at the approaching bus.

"You sure about this one?" Wade asked, his voice low.

"I'm sure," Clem said. His eyes were fixed on the depot. "Her uncle was desperate before he died. That makes her desperate now. We get her to trust me, we get the deed, we sell it to Halverson for a premium."

Wade smirked. "And if she's smart?"

"Smart doesn't matter when you are out of time and out of help," Clem replied, his tone flat. He opened the truck door. "You wait by the post. Signal me when you spot her with the folder. Give me one tap of your boot on the porch. I will signal you back with a brake light flashing twice."

Wade tipped his hat. "Easy money."

Clem climbed in and started the engine. "Only if we do it right. Do not miss the signal."

* * *

MILLIE STEPPED DOWN from the bus with a suitcase in one hand and stubbornness in the other. Exhaustion sat behind her eyes, but she didn't have time for it.

Montana was wide and quiet, and it didn't care who noticed. The air felt different, thinner maybe, and it carried dust the way some places carried humidity, steady and unavoidable. Millie blinked once, then twice, and decided her eyes weren't going to water. Not here. Not now.

Her one suitcase was scuffed at the corners, the latch stubborn enough to need a smack from the heel of her hand. But the other thing she carried mattered more. A folder, thick and tired, tied with string. It was a folder opened too many times, and it always ended the same way.

Behind her, the bus hissed, then it was already gone, leaving her with a gust of grit and the sound of her own breathing. The little depot wasn't much. A bench. A bulletin board with curled notices. A man leaning against the post like he'd been there since the first fence went up. He looked her over, not rude, just curious, the way people did when you weren't part of the scenery.

Millie adjusted her grip on the folder. Tightened the string. Tightened herself.

Her uncle had written three letters before he died. Three. Like he knew he didn't have many left. The first letter had been hopeful. The second one sounded tired. The third was a hurry, written hard and fast, like he didn't have the breath for a fourth.

Millie, I started something I can't finish. You're the only one I trust with it. Don't let them take it. Don't let it vanish.

He hadn't said who "them" was, but the letters had carried a name anyway, like smoke clinging to fabric. A neighbor. A man with land already, but always wanting more. A man who knew how slow paperwork moved and how fast a grieving family could lose their nerve.

Millie wasn't the grieving type. Not in public.

She reached up and smoothed her hair, as if that could smooth the rest of her life. It was pinned back tight for a reason, so the wind wouldn't take it. Her dress was simple, travel-stained, and she'd chosen it for one reason. It didn't wrinkle much. She'd needed that little lie of control.

A red truck rolled past, slow, then slower, then it kept going. She felt the eyes on her back like a hand. She turned just enough to show she noticed, then looked away again, like she didn't care.

The man by the post shifted his weight, spat into the dust without a second thought, then tapped his boot heel once against the wood. Not loud. Not for her. Just enough. Driving by just then, the red truck didn't slow, but its brake lights flashed twice.

Inside the folder was a mess, organized just enough to look official.

A homestead claim. Dates. A rough map drawn by hand. Receipts for supplies her uncle had bought, maybe to prove he'd worked the land. On the map, her uncle had circled the spring twice, hard enough to score the paper. The note beside it was short. *Water holds this place together.* Letters with official stamps that looked important, until you read them and realized they said almost nothing. The words "prove up" appeared more than once, underlined hard, as if her uncle could press the law into obedience with a pencil.

Millie knew the basics. She'd read everything twice. She'd asked questions back home and gotten answers that sounded like shrugs.

A claimant had to live on the land. Improve it. Build something. Work it. Then, if the government believed you, it became yours. It sounded simple when people explained it across a counter. It wasn't simple when the person who started it was buried two states away and all you had was a folder full of notes.

The clock was not polite about it either. If she missed the land office deadline, the claim would go soft, then disappear.

She hadn't come all this way to be pushed around.

Her uncle had been close to finishing. Close enough that it made her angry. Close enough that it made her hopeful.

Hope was dangerous out here. She could feel that already.

A woman came out of the depot office, wiping her hands on her apron like the dust was her fault. She was middle-aged, strong in the shoulders, and she had the look of someone who'd watched a thousand people arrive with dreams, then leave without them.

"You need a room?" the woman asked.

Millie nodded. "Just for a night. I'll check in after I handle some business."

The bus ride had been brutal. She'd slept in pieces through potholes, crying babies, and strangers who didn't know the meaning of quiet. Her body wanted a bed, but her mind stayed on the job in front of her.

The woman tilted her head. "You got family in town?"

"No, ma'am."

"Work?"

Millie hesitated, then decided honesty would cost less than pretending. "Land."

That word changed the air. Not much, just enough. The woman's eyes shifted toward the folder in Millie's hand, then back to her face.

"What kind of land?" she asked, like she already knew there were kinds, and some of them brought trouble with them.

Millie swallowed. "A claim. My uncle's."

The woman's mouth tightened, then relaxed again. "You're late in the season for starting over."

"I didn't come to start over," Millie said. The words came out sharper than she meant. She softened her tone, but not the meaning. "I came to finish."

The woman studied her for a long moment, then agreed like she respected that, or at least understood it.

"You'll want the county office," she said. "And you'll want directions that don't get you lost."

"I'd appreciate both," Millie replied.

The woman wiped her hands again, then pointed. "There's a diner on Main. You can get a hot meal, and you can ask questions without folks pretending they don't hear you. Just don't ask the wrong person."

Millie almost smiled. Almost. "How do I tell the difference?"

The woman gave her a look that held a dry sort of humor. "You won't. Not at first. Just pay attention."

Millie turned her suitcase upright and started toward the street, the folder still tucked tight to her ribs, held close the way you held something you couldn't afford to lose. She'd barely taken three steps when a voice behind her called out. It was quiet, but curious enough to stop her.

"Miss," the man at the post said.

Millie stopped and looked back. He wasn't old, but he had lines like he'd argued with the sun more than once. Hat pulled low, hands relaxed in a way that suggested he didn't waste energy, or words.

He nodded toward the folder, then toward the open land beyond town, like he could see exactly where she was headed.

"You headed out there alone?" he asked.

Millie lifted her chin. "Yes."

He didn't argue. He just watched her a second longer.

"Road doesn't care about brave," he said quietly. "It'll still swallow you."

Millie held his gaze. "Then I'll drive slower."

The man's mouth twitched, not quite a smile, more like approval that tried to pretend it wasn't.

He tipped his hat a fraction. "Suit yourself."

Millie turned away, but she felt his eyes follow her, steady and measuring, as if he'd already started counting her chances.

And, worse, as if he'd already started counting what she might be worth.

Millie didn't look back again.

If she did, she'd have to admit the man had gotten under her skin, and she had no time for that. She had a county office to find, a diner to stomach, and a piece of land waiting out there like a test she didn't get to study for.

Main Street was short and dusty. A few storefronts. A feed store. A diner with a window full of pie that looked like it had been sitting there since breakfast and didn't care who judged it. Millie walked in anyway. She ate, asked a couple careful questions, and listened twice as hard as she spoke. She didn't say "homestead" to just anybody. She said, "my uncle's place" and watched faces, watched pauses, watched the way people answered without answering.

She left with directions that sounded like a riddle and a key detail that sat heavy in her stomach.

"Don't miss the turn," the waitress had said, wiping down the counter like she'd seen too many folks miss it. "If you hit the dry creek bed, you went too far."

Millie nodded like she understood, even though she didn't.

Behind the diner, in an empty lot next to the feed store, a man with a pencil behind his ear rented her a truck that had seen better years and didn't care who knew it. The paint was sun-faded, the seat cracked, and the floorboard held a fine layer of dust that looked like it paid rent. Millie climbed in and set her suitcase on the floorboard. She set the folder on the seat beside her and rested one hand on it for a moment, like it could jump out and run. It started on the second try. The engine shuddered, then settled into a steady rattle that sounded almost confident.

The town fell away behind her. Not dramatically, just quietly, like Montana had a lot of room and didn't waste it on goodbyes.

The land opened up in front of her, and she tried not to show her reaction, even to herself.

It was big. Bigger than she expected. Not just distance, but emptiness. The kind that made you feel small without insulting you. The sky stretched wide and clean, and the light had a sharpness to it.

Millie tightened her grip on the wheel. Her knuckles weren't white, but they were thinking about it.

The first few miles were fine. Hard-packed road, a few scattered fence lines, a couple of cattle that looked up with slow interest and then went back to their business. Millie followed the directions in her head. Left at the leaning cottonwood. Past the old windmill. Keep going until you think you've gone too far.

Then keep going anyway.

The road narrowed. Gravel turned to ruts. Ruts turned to two pale tracks through grass and dirt. The signage, if it had ever existed, gave up and disappeared. The wind picked up, pushing dust across the hood in low sheets. It made the world look like an old faded photograph.

Millie swallowed. She told herself she was fine.

She told herself she'd driven worse.

She told herself a lot of things.

A gust hit the truck broadside and it drifted just enough to make her breath catch. The tires spat gravel. She corrected, too fast, then eased it back. Her heart settled. Her pride did not.

Out here, there were no landmarks that felt friendly. Just land and sky and a road that could vanish if it felt like it.

She slowed. The waitress had said don't miss the turn, but she hadn't said what the turn looked like. Millie watched for anything that might be a sign. A break in the grass. A post. A fence corner. She saw a dry creek bed ahead and felt her stomach drop.

That's when the tire went.

It wasn't a dramatic blowout. It was a sharp crack, then a heavy thump-thump-thump that pulled the wheel hard to the right. Millie fought it, brought the truck down to a crawl, and guided it off onto what looked like the shoulder. Except it wasn't really a shoulder. It was just ground that happened to be a little flatter.

She sat there for a second, both hands on the wheel, breathing through her nose like that could keep her from saying something she'd regret.

Then she got out.

The wind hit her immediately. Dust stung her eyes. She blinked it away and walked around to the front right tire.

Flat.

Of course.

Millie looked up and around like the land might offer an apology. Nothing. No other vehicles. No house. No help. Just the road behind her and the road ahead, and both of them looking equally unconcerned.

She opened the driver's side door and grabbed the folder off the seat. That was instinct. She hated that it was instinct. She set it carefully on the floorboard, tucked under the seat edge, out of the wind and out of sight. Then she popped the hood, as if the hood had anything to do with the tire. She didn't know why she did it. Maybe because it made her feel like she was doing something.

She moved to the back and found the jack. Found the lug wrench. Found the spare, and her first real problem.

The spare was there. It was also bald, worn down like it had been dragged across stone, and the sidewall had a crack that made her stomach tighten.

Millie stared at it, then glanced back toward the flat tire like she might negotiate with it.

No.

She wasn't going back. Not today.

She hooked the bumper jack into place and started pumping the handle. The first few strokes were easy, then it began to click and bite, lifting the truck one stubborn notch at a time. She kept at it until the flat tire hovered just off the dirt.

The lug nuts fought her.

Millie planted her feet, put her weight into the wrench, and pulled. Nothing. She repositioned and pulled again. Still nothing. Her hands slipped and scraped, and she hissed through her teeth, more angry at herself than the truck.

"Come on," she muttered, and leaned into it again.

The wrench finally gave, and the lug nut moved a fraction. Millie exhaled hard like she'd won a small war.

She didn't see the red truck at first.

It came over the rise behind her, slow enough that it didn't throw much dust. Just a low, steady roll like the driver wasn't in a hurry and didn't want to announce himself. It crept closer, then stopped a good distance back.

Millie kept working, but her shoulders tightened.

The driver sat for a moment. Watching.

Then the door opened.

Boots hit the ground. The man who stepped out didn't walk fast. He didn't wave. He took in the road, the sky, the truck, and Millie beside it, like he was looking at a scene that needed decoding.

He approached at an angle, not straight on, and he didn't speak until he was close enough that she could hear him over the wind.

"You're a long way from town for a bad tire," he said.

Millie kept the wrench in her hand. She didn't aim it. She didn't put it down either.

"I'm handling it," she replied.

His gaze dropped, quick and quiet, not lingering. Clean hands with a smear of grease now. Dress hem dusty. A folder on the floorboard, barely visible. He didn't stare at it, but he saw it. His eyes flicked back to her face.

"Looks like it," he said, dry as the dirt. "You got a spare that'll hold?"

Millie straightened, wiped her palm on her skirt without thinking, and instantly regretted it. "It'll have to."

He agreed, like that was an answer he respected.

Relief tried to creep in. Pride stepped on it.

The man looked down the road, then back at her rented truck. "Leave it here. We'll come back with a real tire."

Millie stiffened. "I'm not leaving my truck on the side of the road."

"You already did," he said, calm. "Only difference is, now it won't be your problem alone."

Millie lifted her chin and went back to the lug nuts like she didn't need him, like she hadn't been alone out here two minutes ago with the wind clawing at her nerves.

The man watched her work, calm and quiet, and for the first time since she stepped off that bus, Millie had the distinct feeling that Montana had finally noticed her.

She leaned into the wrench again. The lug nut gave a fraction, then stopped, like it wanted to argue.

Millie set her jaw and pulled harder.

Behind her, the man said nothing. No helpful suggestions. No fake coughing to announce he was still there. Just a steady presence and the sound of wind through the grass.

When the lug nut finally turned, she let out a breath she didn't mean to share.

"Stubborn," the man said.

"So am I," Millie replied, and went back to work.

She got two lug nuts loose. The third one laughed at her. The wrench slipped, her hand slid, and pain flashed across her knuckles. She hissed, shook it once, then grabbed the wrench again like she wasn't going to give the world the satisfaction of watching her bleed.

The man took one step closer.

"I can break it loose," he said.

"I didn't ask."

He nodded like he expected that. He crouched near the tire anyway, not touching anything, just looking.

"You're using your arms," he said. "Put your weight on it. Use your heel."

Millie stared at him. "You always give instructions to strangers on the side of the road?"

"Only the ones who look like they'll throw the wrench at me."

She tightened her grip. "Don't tempt me."

His mouth twitched again, almost a smile, but it didn't reach his eyes. Those stayed careful.

Millie repositioned the wrench, put her foot on it, and leaned down. The lug nut popped loose with a sharp snap that made her heart jump.

She didn't look pleased. She did feel pleased.

The man stood back up. "There you go."

Millie bent and loosened the rest, working faster now, breath steady. She didn't need him. Not technically. Not yet.

But she did need the spare to hold.

She dragged it out, rolled it closer, and her stomach tightened when she saw the cracked sidewall again. A crack that didn't care about hope, or stubbornness, or the fact that she'd come too far.

The man's eyes went to it.

"That won't make it," he said.

"It'll make it to the claim," Millie answered.

"That's not what you need it to do."

Millie straightened. "And what do you think I need?"

He looked past her, down the road she'd come from. Then he glanced toward the horizon where the land lay open and quiet, as if it couldn't hear a thing.

"You need to get back to town," he said. "You need a real tire. And if you're headed where I think you're headed, you need to get there before you lose daylight."

Millie bristled. "I didn't ask for a weather report."

He shook his head, still calm. "No. You didn't."

He walked to his red truck and opened the passenger door, then leaned inside and came out with a tire iron that looked like it had lived through a few bad days. He tossed it lightly from one hand to the other.

"I can help," he said. "But it's not free."

There it was. Not romance. Not charm. Just a transaction, clean and honest.

Millie narrowed her eyes. "What do you want?"

"Gas money," he said, like he'd already decided it was the most reasonable thing in the world. "And a look at the map you're using."

Millie's hand went instinctively toward the folder on the floorboard, like she could cover it with her palm from five feet away.

"No."

He didn't argue. He just watched her, patient, like he'd wait all day if he had to, and that made her more uncomfortable than any pressure.

"I'm not asking for your papers," he said. "I'm asking for the map. You can hold it the whole time."

Millie stared at him. The wind pushed dust between them, and for a second she felt how alone she was out here. Not helpless. Just alone.

She didn't like that feeling. She liked it even less that he knew it.

"How much gas money?" she asked, sharp.

He shrugged. "Enough to make it worth stopping."

"That's not a number."

"It's a negotiation."

Millie let out a slow breath, like she was counting to ten and deciding to stop at six.

"How much?" she asked.

He didn't glance at her purse. He didn't glance anywhere that would look greedy. He just leaned against his red truck and let the wind do the talking for him.

"Five dollars," he said.

Millie laughed once, short and sharp, like the sound surprised even her. "For what, exactly? A conversation and a tire iron?"

"For stopping," he said. "For turning around. For the miles. For the fact that you're not walking."

"That's not gas money," she said.

"It's gas," he replied, "and it's my time."

Millie narrowed her eyes. "Your time must be precious."

He shrugged, calm as ever. "Depends on who's asking for it."

"I didn't ask," she reminded him.

"No," he said, "but you're thinking about it."

Millie stared at him a long moment. Then she reached into her purse and drew out bills one at a time, slow, like she wanted him to feel every second of it.

She held up four dollars. Not hidden. Not folded. Four clean bills pinched between two fingers.

"That's what I've got for gas," she said. "Take it or keep driving."

He looked at the money, then at her face, like he was weighing more than the bills.

For a moment, Millie thought he might leave. Thought he might try to make her blink first.

Instead, he reached out and took the four dollars without brushing her fingers. Quick, careful. Like manners still mattered, even out here.

"All right," he said, pocketing it. "Four."

Millie didn't relax. She didn't thank him.

But something in her shifted anyway, just a hair. Not trust. Not yet.

He wasn't a saint.

Which, oddly, made him feel safer than one.

"Now the map," he said.

Millie hesitated, then slid the folder out and untied the string. She didn't hand it over. She opened it herself, flipped to the rough page with her uncle's penciled lines, and held it up so he could see.

The man leaned in, but not too close. His eyes moved quick, taking in the road marks, the creek bed, the circled spring.

"County won't care how hard you want it," he said. "They'll bounce you if your dates don't match their book."

Millie went still. That sounded too true.

"I need the county office," she admitted, and hated that she'd said it out loud.

He nodded, already knowing. "Then you need to get back to town first."

Millie lifted her chin. "I'm not turning around."

The man's gaze held steady, and in it she saw something that looked like calculation, but also something else, buried under it.

"You will," he said, quiet and sure. "You just haven't realized it yet."

Millie snugged every loosened lug back down before she lowered the rented truck off the jack and locked it. She grabbed her suitcase and the folder, then hesitated long enough to hate herself for hesitating.

The man opened the passenger door of his red truck and stepped back, giving her space, leaving the choice where it belonged.

She climbed in anyway.

She noticed it the moment she climbed into his red truck. He didn't bark orders, didn't act like he owned the road, didn't treat her like a problem to be managed. He just drove. Steady hands. Eyes always up. Like the land could change its mind at any moment and he'd rather be ready than surprised.

Millie sat stiff in the passenger seat with her folder on her lap, one arm wrapped around it like it might try to escape. Her rented truck was still out there behind them, sitting lopsided in the dirt like a bad decision. Millie tried not to think about it. Every mile back to town felt like she was leaving something exposed.

"You always carry paperwork like it's gold?" the man asked, voice dry, not looking at her.

"It's not paperwork," Millie said.

He glanced over once, quick, then back to the road. "That a fact?"

"It's my uncle's life," she replied, and immediately wished she hadn't given him that much.

The man didn't smile. He didn't soften either. He just nodded, filing the information away in a drawer he kept locked.

Then he surprised her.

He stuck out his hand, more business than kindness. His palm was rough, knuckles scarred in the quiet way of work.

"Name's Spyker," he said. "Clement Spyker, but folks just call me Clem."

Millie looked at his hand for a second too long. Out here, a handshake could mean anything. A deal. A promise. A trap.

She gave him her hand anyway, firm enough to make her point.

"Mildred Caldwell," she said. Millie was for family, and for the version of herself that still lived back home. "You can call me Mildred."

Clem's grip was brief, polite, and gone before it could turn familiar. His eyes stayed on her a second, then went back to the road.

"Mildred," he repeated, like he was testing whether the name fit her.

He put his eyes back on the road. "You headed to the claim first, or you trying to straighten the papers before you go?"

Millie didn't answer right away.

"County office closes early," he said. "If you're trying to get anything done, you'll want to move."

Millie watched the road. "I'm moving."

"No," he said. "You're riding."

She shot him a look. "You like correcting people?"

"I like people staying out of trouble," he answered.

Millie almost laughed at that. Almost. It didn't sound like concern. It sounded like experience.

CHAPTER TWO

TOWN, EYES, AND QUIET MEASURING

They rolled into town as if nothing had happened, as if she hadn't been stranded on a road that barely existed.

Clem didn't pull up in front of the courthouse first. He drove past it as if it were an afterthought, then eased the truck into a spot near the feed store and killed the engine.

"We're getting you a real tire," he said.

"I'm going to the county office," Millie replied.

Clem's head turned just enough for her to feel it. "You can do both."

"I don't have time."

"You don't have a choice."

Millie opened her mouth, then shut it. She hated that he was right.

Clem stepped out and walked around to her side. Not to open the door for her. He didn't do that kind of polite. He just stood there like he was waiting for her to keep up.

Millie left the suitcase in the truck and climbed out, smoothing her skirt, folder still in hand. The moment she hit the sidewalk, she felt it again. Eyes.

Not open staring. Just the quiet kind. The kind that measured you, then decided where you belonged.

Clem nodded to a man outside the feed store. "Afternoon, Wade."

Wade tipped his hat without smiling. Then, without Millie noticing he tapped his boot heel once against the wood. "Clem."

Not friendly. Not hostile. Familiar in the way of two men who'd seen each other do things and never bothered asking questions.

Clem kept walking. Millie followed.

Clem didn't turn toward the courthouse steps.

Millie stopped. "That's where I need to be."

He kept moving. He just turned his head enough for her to see his profile. "In a minute."

"I don't have a minute."

He looked at her then, calm as a man with nothing to lose. "You do if you want to get seen before you get swallowed."

Millie blinked. "What does that even mean?"

"It means the county office doesn't run on clocks," he said, still walking. "It runs on people. I need to know who's working the counter today, and I need to know who's got tires."

Millie hated that it made sense.

Clem angled toward the diner, following a plan he'd already drawn out in his head.

"Two minutes," he said. "Then we go."

The bell above the door gave a tired jingle. The smell hit Millie first, coffee and fried food, and something sweet in the back that made her stomach remember she was human. Clem didn't even glance at the pie case.

He wasn't here to eat. He was here to be seen, and to listen.

A few heads turned. Not because Millie walked in, but because Clem did. Some faces held neutral. One or two went flat. Everybody recognized him, even if they didn't like him.

Behind the counter, the same waitress looked up and didn't bother hiding what she thought.

"Well," she said, wiping her hands on her apron, "if it isn't trouble on two legs."

Clem's mouth curved like he was amused against his will. "Hello to you too, Doris."

Doris's eyes slid to Millie, then straight to the folder, like the string had a bell on it. Her mouth tightened a fraction.

"Well, look who didn't make it far," she said. "You find that turn?"

"I found trouble first," Millie said.

Doris looked back at Clem. "You picking up stranded travelers now?"

"Her name's Mildred," Clem said, like he'd decided that was enough. "She's in from out of town."

Doris lifted a brow. "Out of town is a wide place."

Millie kept her voice flat. "I'm here on business."

"Everybody's here on business," Doris said, and poured coffee with the weight of a punishment.

Clem leaned an elbow on the counter, casual, like he had all day. Millie could feel the performance. She could also feel the room watching her, sizing her up without anyone raising their voice.

Clem kept his voice low. "Who's working the county counter today?"

Doris snorted. "If you're asking, you already know."

"I want to hear it anyway."

Doris poured the coffee and slid it toward him. "Mrs. Raskin. And she's in a mood. Been in a mood since Tuesday."

Clem nodded like he'd just been handed a piece of the puzzle. "What about the tire shop?"

"Earl's got a shipment," Doris said. "If you're lucky."

Clem set a coin on the counter. "Coffee."

Doris looked at the coin and didn't touch it. "You paying for her too?"

Millie opened her mouth.

Clem said, "No."

It came out quick. Firm. Not unkind, just final.

Millie blinked at him.

Clem added, casual as breath, "She can speak for herself."

Doris studied him, then Millie, then cocked her head like she approved of the boundary.

Millie didn't thank him. She wasn't sure if it was manners or strategy.

Probably both.

Doris looked back to Millie. "So what kind of business brings you in with Clem Spyker?"

Millie felt the room lean in, quiet as a shadow.

She chose her words carefully. "My uncle filed a claim. I'm here to finish it."

The word claim landed heavy.

At the far end of the counter, a man stirring his coffee went still. Not dramatic. Just still. Like he'd heard something he didn't want to hear and couldn't pretend otherwise.

Clem didn't turn his head. He didn't look at the man. But Millie saw a small shift in Clem's posture, a minute tightening, like he'd just confirmed something he'd been listening for.

Doris's eyes softened a fraction. "Honey, that's a hard kind of business."

Millie kept her face steady. "I didn't come all this way for easy."

Clem lifted the coffee, took one sip, and set it down.

"Two minutes," he said again, more to the room than to her. Then he looked at Millie. "Let's go get you a tire, then we'll go see Mrs. Raskin."

Clem didn't waste time after the diner.

He walked Millie straight back outside like the place had

served its purpose. Two minutes, just like he promised. Doris watched them go with a look that wasn't a blessing, but wasn't a curse either.

"Earl's," Clem was already moving.

Millie followed, folder hugged to her ribs, trying not to look like she'd been taken in by the town's most questionable guide. The street felt smaller now, not because the buildings had moved, but because she could feel eyes tracking them. Not a single voice raised. Not a single hand pointed. Just quiet attention.

Earl's tire shop sat a half block off Main, all grease smell and sun-baked rubber. Earl himself looked up from a counter covered in parts, took one look at Clem, and sighed like he'd been expecting him since breakfast.

"Clem," Earl said.

"Earl."

That was the whole greeting. Not friendly. Not unfriendly. The exchange men used when they'd seen each other in bad moments and decided it was best to stay on speaking terms.

Clem nodded toward Millie's folder, then away. "Need a tire, already mounted if you've got one. Fast."

Earl's eyes flicked to Millie, then to the folder, then back to Clem. He didn't ask questions. He just jerked his chin toward the garage.

"Sure. I've got one mounted already," he said. "If you're paying."

Millie started to speak.

Clem cut in. "She's paying. We'll trade in the rim later."

Millie pulled bills from her purse, counted them once, then again like she didn't trust Montana math. Earl took the money without smiling. Two minutes later the tire was loaded into Clem's truck bed, tied down like it mattered.

Millie noticed her hands were shaking, just slightly, as she retied the string on her folder.

"Now," Clem said, "county."

The courthouse was nearby. Plain, square, and stubborn. A building that didn't care about your intentions. It cared about paper.

Inside, the air smelled like floor wax and old ink. A couple of benches. A railing. A counter with a glass partition that made everything feel like a transaction, even breathing.

Mrs. Raskin was exactly what Doris had promised. Not evil. Not kind. Just tired, and rigid, and shaped by too many people who thought rules were optional.

Her hair was pulled back tight. Her reading glasses sat low on her nose. Her hands moved with the practiced irritation of someone who had stamped a thousand forms and never once been thanked for it.

She looked up. Her eyes went to Clem first, then to Millie.

"Mr. Spyker," she said. Not a greeting, a fact.

"Mrs. Raskin," Clem replied. Polite. Controlled. Familiar.

Millie didn't like that.

Mrs. Raskin's gaze shifted to Millie. "Can I help you?"

Millie stepped forward. "My name is Mildred Caldwell. My uncle filed a claim. I'm here to finish the paperwork."

Mrs. Raskin's eyes dropped to the folder, then back to Millie's face. "Homestead?"

Millie hesitated. Just a fraction.

Clem didn't.

"She's here on a claim filed by her uncle," he said. "She needs the file pulled."

Mrs. Raskin's mouth tightened. "I asked her."

Millie swallowed. "Yes. Homestead."

Mrs. Raskin sat straighter, like that answered a question she already knew the outcome of. She reached for a ledger, flipped it open with an irritated thumb, then ran a finger down the page.

"You said your uncle filed it," she repeated.

"Yes, ma'am."

"What is his name?"

Millie gave it. Mrs. Raskin wrote something down, then stood, disappeared into the back, and returned with a thin file that looked too small to hold a life.

She set it on the counter with a soft thud and opened it like she already disliked what she was about to find.

Mrs. Raskin flipped through papers. One. Two. Three. She paused, then flipped back. Her finger tapped a blank spot as if it had insulted her.

Then she looked up.

"Your uncle's file isn't complete," she said.

Millie felt the words hit her like a shove. "It is. I have the papers."

Mrs. Raskin lifted a hand, not unkind, just final. "There is a deadline on proving up."

Millie leaned forward. "He was close. He was almost done."

"Almost done is not done," Mrs. Raskin said. "And a death does not pause the requirement."

Millie's stomach clenched. She untied the folder with fingers that wanted to shake and refused to.

She slid papers through the gap at the bottom of the glass. Receipts. Notes. A hand-drawn map. A letter with a stamp. A piece of paper with her uncle's handwriting so familiar it made her throat burn.

Mrs. Raskin didn't react to the handwriting. She reacted to dates.

She lined them up. Moved one aside. Moved another. Her finger tapped again, that same blank spot.

"This affidavit is missing," she said.

Millie stared. "Affidavit?"

Mrs. Raskin looked at her over the glasses. "The witness statement verifying residence and improvements."

"He lived there," Millie said, too sharp. "He built on it. He worked it. He…"

Mrs. Raskin didn't flinch. "Do you have a signed witness statement?"

Millie opened her mouth, then closed it.

She didn't.

Mrs. Raskin continued, voice still flat. "Your improvements list is incomplete. Your residence dates do not match what's in our ledger. And the water rights notation here is… vague."

Millie's heart thudded once, heavy.

Water. The spring.

Mrs. Raskin glanced down again. "This claim hinges on that spring, correct?"

Millie swallowed. "It's on the property."

"And it is marked as a shared source in older records," Mrs. Raskin said. "Which means the access and usage must be clearly stated. Otherwise, it becomes contested."

Contested.

Millie felt her hands go cold. She pushed more papers forward like effort could fill the missing pieces.

Mrs. Raskin looked at them, then slid two back.

"These do not help," she said. "These are notes."

"They're his notes," Millie replied, the edge in her voice she couldn't stop.

Mrs. Raskin's expression didn't change. "I understand what they are. I'm telling you what they are not."

Millie stood there, outnumbered by a counter and a ledger and rules she hadn't written.

Clem had stayed back, arms loose, posture calm. Like he was only there as a witness to her stubbornness.

Then Millie made the mistake of reaching for one paper, pointing to a date and trying to argue it.

Mrs. Raskin shut the file halfway.

Not slammed. Just closed enough to signal the end.

"That is not how this works," she said. "You do not argue the ledger. You match it."

Millie went still. She could feel the trap now. Not a trap set by Mrs. Raskin, exactly. A trap set by the system. Paper or nothing. Dates or nothing. Signatures or nothing.

And time.

Clem stepped forward.

Not fast. Not aggressive. Just one measured step that changed the balance.

"Mrs. Raskin," he said, "what's the fastest way for her to cure the file?"

Mrs. Raskin's eyes shifted to him. "That depends on whether she can produce the missing affidavit and whether she can show proof of improvements."

"She can," Clem said, and it sounded like a promise he hadn't earned the right to make.

Millie snapped her head toward him. "I can?"

Clem didn't look at her. Not yet. "If we get eyes on the property, we can list improvements properly. If she can find a witness who will sign, we can address the affidavit."

Mrs. Raskin's mouth tightened again, but this time it wasn't irritation. It was consideration, the kind that hurt more because it was almost fair.

"Even if she does," Mrs. Raskin said, "a contest can be filed."

As if summoned by the word, the front door opened.

A man stepped in like he belonged there.

He was clean. Confident. Hat in hand. Boots polished enough to tell a story. He smiled at Mrs. Raskin with the ease of someone who had smiled in this building before.

"Mrs. Raskin," he said warmly. "Hope I'm not interrupting."

Mrs. Raskin's face didn't warm back. "Mr. Halverson."

Millie's stomach dropped. She didn't know him, but she knew the name. Halverson. It was in her uncle's letters. A neighbor, he'd written, a man with land already, and an appetite for more.

The man's gaze moved to Millie, then to her folder, then to Clem. The smile didn't change.

"I couldn't help overhearing," Halverson said, polite as church. "Homestead matter?"

Millie felt heat rise in her chest. "This is private."

Halverson's smile stayed in place. "Of course. I only mean, some folks have interests out near that spring. Water is... valuable. Access is... tricky."

He said it like he was discussing weather. Like he wasn't threatening anything at all.

Millie gripped the folder so hard her fingers ached.

Mrs. Raskin looked down at the file, then back up. "Mr. Halverson, are you filing a contest?"

"Not today," he said. "I'm simply making sure everyone understands the landscape. A claim is a claim, until it isn't. Folks don't like surprises."

Millie's mind snapped back to her uncle's letters, the ones that read like warnings. Halverson. A man who didn't stop at his own fence line.

She realized, all at once, that she wasn't just finishing paperwork.

She was stepping into a fight she hadn't met yet.

Clem's voice stayed even. "She'll have her paperwork right."

Halverson's eyes flicked to Clem, amused. "Will she?"

Clem didn't rise to it. He turned slightly toward Millie, lowering his voice like he was giving her an exit ramp.

"Here's what you do," he said. "You get eyes on the property. Today. You list every improvement. Fence line, dwelling, well work, whatever is there. You find someone who saw your uncle living there, someone who'll sign. I'll handle the filings while you move."

Millie stared at him. "You'll handle the filings."

"Temporary," Clem said. "Necessary. Time is the enemy."

Mrs. Raskin watched them, tired and rigid and not blind. "If you do that," she said to Millie, "bring it back fast. Do not wait."

Halverson's smile thinned. "And if you can't," he added gently, "someone else will."

Millie's pulse pounded once, hard.

She looked at her folder. Then at Clem. Then at the courthouse door, like she could already see the property out there waiting, silent and indifferent.

Millie lifted her chin.

"All right," she said.

Clem's eyes sharpened, just slightly, like he'd been waiting for that word. His mouth moved, but she couldn't hear him. Under his breath, almost to himself, he said, "Stay fed, stay ahead, don't get soft."

"Good," he replied, calm as ever. "Then we move."

CHAPTER THREE

THE FENCE LINE

Millie followed Clem out of the courthouse like the building had spat her back onto the sidewalk.

The sun felt too bright after the stale air inside. Her ears still rang with Mrs. Raskin's flat voice, and that polite man's smile. Mr. Halverson. Clean boots. Clean hands. A man who didn't lift a shovel, but somehow ended up owning the shovel.

Millie tightened her grip on the folder until her fingers hurt.

Clem didn't let her drift. He angled them toward the side of the building where the wind cut cleaner, away from the benches and the small crowd that always formed near any door that mattered. He stopped beside his truck and faced her like he was about to lay out terms.

"You heard her," he said. "We don't have time to argue."

"I wasn't arguing," Millie snapped.

Clem's eyes held steady. "You were losing."

That landed hard. Millie hated that it was true.

She stood straighter. "I can fix it."

"You can," Clem said. "But you can't fix it fast if you're running back and forth every time they need a paper pulled."

Millie's mouth tightened. "So what, you're going to do it for me out of the goodness of your heart?"

Clem didn't blink. "No."

At least he was honest.

He reached into the glove box and pulled out a small stack of forms that looked folded and unfolded enough to memorize. He handed them over without flourish, more tool than trap.

"It's a limited power of attorney," he said. "Specific."

Millie stared down at the paper, then back up at him. "I'm not signing my land away."

"You're not," Clem said. "Read it."

Millie did.

The words were printed plain, language meant to sound harmless. Limited. Temporary. For the purpose of filing and retrieving documents only. The dates were blank. Her name line waited like a dare.

"I can only file and retrieve documents for you," Clem said, voice even. "Nothing else."

Millie looked at him. "And if I say no?"

Clem's gaze flicked toward the courthouse doors. "Then you go back in there alone, and every time she needs something, you lose a half day. Halverson will file before you're finished being stubborn."

She hated that he used her word.

The courthouse was edging toward closing when Mrs. Raskin appeared in the doorway, like she'd been watching the whole time. She walked over, not hurried, not curious. Just tired.

"What is this?" she asked.

Clem handed her the top page. "Limited power of attorney. Filing and retrieval only."

Mrs. Raskin adjusted her glasses and scanned it. Her eyes moved fast, practiced. Then she looked at Millie.

"You understand what you're signing?" she asked.

Millie's pulse thudded once. "I understand I'm running out of time."

"That is not an answer," Mrs. Raskin said, firm, not cruel.

Millie met her eyes. "He will not sell anything. He will not lease anything. He will not touch my land. He will only file and retrieve documents."

Mrs. Raskin nodded. "That is what it says."

Clem didn't smile. He didn't look pleased. He just reached into his pocket and produced a pen like he'd been carrying it for exactly this moment.

Millie took it and held it between her fingers. The point hovered over her name.

One sharp question rose up, and she didn't soften it.

"If you do anything outside that limit," she said to Clem, "what happens?"

Clem's eyes didn't flinch. "You revoke it."

"And if I'm out on the property and you're in town?"

"Then you come back and revoke it," he said. "And if you want it in writing, we can add a line that says you can revoke it at any time, for any reason."

Mrs. Raskin's mouth tightened, almost approving. "He's correct."

Millie looked down at the paper again. She could feel her uncle's letters in her purse like a weight. Close enough to finishing. Close enough to lose it all.

She signed.

The ink went down smooth and dark. When it dried, something in her loosened, just a fraction.

Relief.

He took the paper back without touching her fingers. He glanced at the signature, then reached into the stack and pulled out a second copy.

"We'll make two," he said.

Mrs. Raskin nodded like this was normal. "One stays with the file. One stays with you."

Clem made sure Millie got the copy she could see. Then, while she was still looking at her own signature like it belonged to someone else, he slipped the other into his inside pocket, flat and careful, like it mattered more than it should.

He didn't gloat.

He didn't say, "Good choice."

* * *

HE WENT QUIET, eyes on the courthouse door, already thinking three steps ahead.

It was too easy, and he didn't like the part of himself that enjoyed it.

He'd planned control, not ruin. Ruin was loud. Control was paperwork.

* * *

MILLIE TUCKED her copy into the folder. She retied the string like it could hold the world together.

Then she looked up at Clem and said, low and firm, "This doesn't mean I trust you."

Clem's gaze met hers, unreadable.

"No," he said. "It means you want to win."

Clem didn't wait for her to feel good about any of it.

He walked her to the truck, opened the passenger door, and stepped back like he was keeping his hands clean. Millie climbed in with her folder clutched on her lap.

The courthouse shrank behind them. The town followed. Then there was only road again, and wind, and that wide Montana sky that made a person feel small even when they were trying hard not to.

Clem drove like he'd been born with a steering wheel in his hands. No hurry. No showing off. Just steady, like the land had taught him that speed was how you ended up in a ditch.

Millie stared out the window and tried to keep her thoughts in a straight line.

She had signed something she never would have signed back home. She could feel the weight of it in her folder, like the ink was still wet and watching her.

"Your truck," Clem said after a while, eyes on the road. "We'll swap that tire, then you can follow me out."

Millie didn't answer right away. Clem didn't push. He didn't ask why she was quiet. He just let the silence sit between them like a third passenger.

When they got back to the rented truck, the tire change went quick. Clem worked without drama. A few controlled movements, a couple of grunts of effort, then the new tire was on like it had always been meant to be there. Millie watched his hands more than she meant to. He moved like a man who didn't waste energy. Nothing extra. Nothing sloppy.

He wiped his palms on a rag, nodded toward the driver's seat. "You're good."

Millie climbed in, started the engine, and followed his red truck out of town.

The road stretched, then thinned, then turned into two pale tracks again. The wind kicked up dust in low sheets, and the land opened wider with every mile.

Then the creek appeared.

Not a roaring thing, not dramatic. Just a ribbon of water catching sunlight, glinting where it shouldn't have been possible. Water that looked like it belonged somewhere else. A quiet miracle, sitting there, not trying to impress anyone.

Millie felt her breath catch.

At a wide spot in the road Clem's red truck slowed down, and Millie pulled alongside him. Her eyes tracked the water, the grass around it, the way the ground dipped and held it like a secret.

Clem saw her staring.

"It's… smaller than I expected," she said, even though that wasn't what she meant at all.

Clem's mouth was almost amused. "Sure."

Millie's cheeks warmed. "I'm just saying."

"I heard you," he replied.

They drove on, the water staying in view longer than it should, then slipping behind a rise. Millie's fingers tightened on the wheel.

She realized it then, all at once, like a truth that had been waiting for her to notice it.

She didn't just want the claim.

She wanted the land.

Millie stopped the rented truck and stepped out. She stood there a moment, just looking. The creek. The grass bending in the wind. The emptiness that somehow felt full.

* * *

CLEM WATCHED HER CAREFULLY. Not her face exactly. Her posture. The way she leaned forward a fraction, like the land had whispered something and she was trying to hear it better. The way she breathed it in, slow, like she could take ownership just by taking a good look.

Her attention hooked onto the property, already half claiming it, and he saw the leverage in that immediately. It made her predictable. It made him… not.

He'd dealt with desperate people before. Loud people. Greedy people. People who wanted things because they wanted them.

This was different.

Millie wanted the land the way a person wanted a home. Not the house, the belonging.

It should've made her easier to play.

Instead, it made something shift in him, small and unwelcome. It wasn't romance, or anything soft; it was a quick awareness, sharp as a breath caught too fast.

He noticed the line of her neck when she turned. The way the wind tugged at her hair, and she didn't bother fixing it. The steadiness in her face, like she'd already decided she wasn't leaving.

Clem didn't like it.

He didn't like noticing.

He didn't like that the thought landed so clean in his head.

She's pretty.

And worse, it wasn't pretty in a way that faded when the light changed.

He looked away, like he could lock the feeling back up where it belonged.

This wasn't him.

Not the Clem he knew.

* * *

SHE CLIMBED BACK into the truck, started the engine, and followed his red taillights again.

They continued a bit longer and then Clem eased his truck to a stop near a fence line.

Millie pulled up behind him and cut the engine. The wind filled the silence immediately, pushing dust along the ground in little restless swirls.

Clem got out and stood still for a moment, looking ahead.

Then he said, almost to himself, "We've got a problem."

Millie climbed out fast. "What?"

Clem didn't answer right away. He just lifted one arm and pointed.

Fresh stakes in the dirt.

A new line, not matching the old fence. Too straight. Too recent. A posted sign flapping in the wind, proud of itself.

NO TRESPASSING.

Millie's stomach dropped, then hardened into something else.

"That's not theirs," she said, voice low.

Clem's eyes stayed on the sign. His face gave nothing away.

"No," he said quietly. "But somebody wants it to be."

Millie took a step forward like she could undo it with sheer will. Her hands curled into fists.

She didn't come all this way to be pushed around.

And Clem, standing beside her, calm as ever, looked like a man who'd been expecting this all along.

Millie turned back to him, her eyes sharp with anger and something close to panic. Before she could think better of it, she reached for his hand.

Not delicate. Not flirtatious. Just human.

Her fingers wrapped around his, warm and sure, like she was grabbing the only solid thing in a shifting world.

"We can fix this," she said, low. Then, softer, like she surprised herself, "Can't we?"

* * *

WE.

The word landed in Clem harder than the sign ever could. He'd been a lot of things in a lot of towns, but he wasn't anybody's we. Not for long. Not on purpose.

He squeezed her hand once, brief and controlled, then let go like he hadn't needed it.

His eyes stayed on the fresh stakes. His voice stayed even.

"We can," he said. "But it won't be clean."

Millie nodded like she'd accept ugly if it meant winning. "Fine."

Clem looked at her then, really looked, and felt that shift again, deeper this time. Not want. Not softness.

Something like responsibility.

He didn't ask for it. He didn't like it.

But it was there.

He turned back to the fence line, unreadable as stone.

"Let's go," he said quietly. "Before they get any farther."

MILLIE WATCHED him turn toward the fence line, and she didn't know why her hand still remembered his. But she knew this much, she wasn't leaving. Not now.

CHAPTER FOUR

NO TRESPASSING

The room the depot lady lined up for Millie was more college dorm than hotel. One narrow bed, a dresser that leaned on an uneven leg, and a window that looked out at nothing in particular. Millie had seen rough on the bus ride west, but this was a new category of rough. Still, it was clean, and it was a bed. And the simple edible meal provided that evening was appreciated after her long day. She saved a few bites for breakfast in the morning.

Her daddy's voice drifted up like it always did when she tried to complain. *You don't know nuttin' while you are sleepin'.*

The only real advantage was location. Back home, "close" meant you could walk. In Montana, "close" meant you only had to drive thirty minutes instead of losing half a day to dirt roads and stubborn distance.

But she wasn't staying here long. Just one night, if that. Not if she had any pride left in her bones.

She drove out before sunrise in the rented truck, when the sky was still pale and undecided. The truck's headlights cut a narrow tunnel through the dust hanging low over the road. Montana was quiet at that hour, not asleep exactly, just listening.

The first thing she noticed was the gate.

It wasn't how she'd left it.

The chain was looped different, tighter, and the hinge squealed like it hadn't squealed yesterday.

Her uncle had fenced what he could, a pen near the shack, a run behind the shed, practical lines for animals and work. But the real boundary out here wasn't wire, it was water.

Millie slowed, hand still on the wheel, eyes moving the way her father had taught her, left to right, near to far. Nothing moved. No birds lifting off the fence. Just wind sliding through grass and bringing dust with it like a habit.

Then she saw the signs.

The *No Trespassing* signs.

The signs weren't on her uncle's fences. They were planted in a straight line toward the creek, like someone had drawn a new border and dared her to argue.

She and Clem had pulled every last one of them down like they were weeds. He'd said it plain, the way he said most things: "If it's your land, you don't need a sign to tell you so." They'd stacked the boards in the back of the truck. That had felt like progress, like claiming something with your own hands.

Now those signs were back up, hammered into the ground as if they'd never been touched. Not one, not two, but a whole line of them, marching along like soldiers that didn't know the war was over.

A note was tacked to the nearest sign, pinned with a nail that still looked bright.

STAY OFF MY PROPERTY!

The handwriting was sharp and angry, the ink pressed hard enough to bite through the paper. Millie stared at it a moment too long, then made herself look away. That was how fear got you, by taking your eyes off everything else.

A tingle crawled up the back of her neck, small and ugly, like a warning bell you couldn't shut off. She listened.

Nothing.

No boot scuff. No cough. No engine idling somewhere behind a hill. Still, she could feel it, that sense of eyes on her, fixed and patient.

She ran her fingers along the wire behind the shed and found the cut, clean and deliberate. Not the boundary fence, just a working fence, the kind that kept animals where they belonged. Someone had cut it anyway.

It wasn't damage. It was a message.

She told herself it was ranch stuff. Weather did strange things. Men did careless things. Fences got worked on and worked over. Signs went up and came down. That was life out here.

Her gut disagreed.

She started walking the boundary anyway, because standing still felt like surrender. The land rolled out around her, wide and quiet, not friendly, not cruel, just there. Dust clung to her shoes. The wind pushed at her skirt like it wanted to turn her back toward town.

Every few yards she found something small, something off. A gate latch turned the wrong direction. A footprint where it shouldn't be. Another dark line on another post, spaced like someone was measuring.

Millie stopped and looked out over the property, over the creek line, the bend of cottonwoods, the raw stretch of ground that could be a ranch if a person fought hard enough for it.

And that was when it hit her, clean and cold.

This wasn't only about land, or water, or dust. It wasn't even about money, not at the center of it.

It was about permission.

About who got to stand here and say, *Mine*.

Millie drew in a slow breath and held it, then let it go slow, like she was steadying her hands before a hard job. Unease sat in her chest, pride right beside it. And if she was honest, there it was too, the first pinch of fear, small but real.

Not enough to send her running.

Enough to tell her a decision was coming, and it needed to happen today.

She walked to the makeshift barn and climbed into her uncle's truck, hopeful. She turned the key. Nothing. Not even a cough.

Again.

Still nothing.

Millie tried the old tricks she'd watched men do a hundred times. They would pump the gas, turn the key slow, then fast. She said something stern under her breath like the engine might get embarrassed and cooperate. The truck stayed dead, polite as a gravestone.

She popped the hood and stared at the tangle of metal as if it were written in a foreign language. She moved a wire. Then another. She might as well have been rearranging spaghetti.

The tractor was worse. It groaned once, then quit, like it had reconsidered the whole idea of work.

She stepped back and noticed the roof. Blue sky winked through gaps between boards. That wasn't "rustic." That was "rain comes in sideways."

Her uncle had thrown together a crude shack on the property, a rough structure that made you think twice about sitting down without checking for nails first. The roof looked like it had survived by luck and patching. Still, it was on the land, and the agreement said that she had to be on the land. Millie had learned long ago that rules only mattered when you followed them first.

Now was the time to inspect it closer. If the land was going to fight her, the shack would too. A few boards along the porch were loose, and the door stuck like it hadn't decided if she belonged. Inside, dust sat on everything like it owned the place. The air smelled stale, like old wood. She dusted off a chair at the table with her hand and sat down to eat last night's leftovers. But she needed water. Millie set her jaw and went straight to the hand pump at the sink.

She worked the handle.
Nothing.
She worked it harder.
Still nothing.

A cold thought slid in. No water meant no cooking, no cleaning, no staying. Not for long. A person could be stubborn, but a person couldn't be stubborn and thirsty.

She went outside and walked the line of pipes, following them like a trail. The morning was already warming up, the sun making the dust bright and sharp. The pipes led her to the pump setup, and it didn't take a mechanic to see trouble. The housing looked tired, bolts rusted, and the whole thing sat there like it had given up last year and nobody noticed.

Millie found a toolbox, thanked her uncle out loud for once, and set to work.

The first nut didn't move.

The second one laughed at her, at least that's what it felt like.

She braced her foot, leaned her weight into the wrench, and pulled until her shoulder burned. The nut finally gave, but not the way she needed. It stripped, slick and ruined, the wrench slipping off, tired of her too.

Millie stared at it, breathing hard. Sweat crawled down her spine. Her hands were shaking, part anger, part plain fatigue. She realized she hadn't had a drink since before sunrise, and now there was no water anywhere but the creek. She looked toward it, then away, taking it personally.

The land stretched out in every direction, wide and unmoved by her effort. It didn't care what she wanted. It didn't care what she deserved. It was just there, bigger than her, older than her, and it could outwait her without trying.

Millie pressed her palm to her ribs and felt it, that ticking, steady and sharp, like a clock somebody had hidden inside her body.

Determination was still there. But it had a crack in it now.

And through that crack came the truth she hated most.
She needed help.

* * *

SHE HEARD his red truck before she saw it. If she was honest, her first thought wasn't, *Who is that?* It was, *Please let that be Clem.* And just as she hoped, the truck rolled into view, red paint dusty, tires chewing gravel, arriving at the exact wrong time and the exact right time. Like he'd been watching the road for her dust, not the other way around.

Clem stepped out with a toolbox in one hand like he could read her mind, and her need for help. He stood there a moment with one hand in his pocket, calm as if he'd been on the property all morning. Then he walked slowly over to the pump where Millie was struggling. He wore an old field jacket, faded to that in between color the sun gives things. On his left lapel sat a small red enamel pin, scuffed, the kind a man might keep even after he stopped talking about where he'd been.

She'd seen one before. Not up close, but enough to recognize it from men who came back from the war and tried to look like nothing had happened.

"That's from overseas," she said, nodding at the pin.

Clem glanced down like he'd forgotten it was there. "Honorable service. That's what it was called."

Millie swallowed. "So, you were in it."

"I was," he said, simple. Then he crouched beside the pump, ran his fingers over the stripped nut, and made a quiet sound that wasn't quite a sigh. "You've got grit in the threads, and you've got the wrong leverage."

He didn't talk while he worked. He just worked. He grunted once, then swapped his wrench angle, worrying the damaged edges like he'd seen worse. He cleaned the threads, set the wrench the right way, and used a short length of pipe for leverage, easy and practiced. In less than fifteen minutes the pump coughed, then surged, and water ran as if it had been waiting for him to show up and set things right. Millie watched every move, taking note, determined to learn this life even if it fought her.

That was when she noticed him, really noticed him. Tall, strong, quiet, blunt. Not showy. Not trying to impress. Still, he'd shown up with exactly what she needed, and that meant he'd been thinking about her.

Clem was almost done when his eyes went past her shoulder, scanning the fence line, the gate, the empty stretch beyond the cottonwoods. The No Trespassing signs were back up. He wasn't nervous, not jumpy, just aware.

"You weren't just Army," Millie said. "Not the usual kind, anyway."

Clem's mouth tightened, just a fraction. "What's the usual kind?"

"The kind that doesn't look at a pasture like it might shoot back."

For a moment he didn't speak. Then he said, "I did some work people didn't talk about."

Millie took a breath. "I've heard of the OSS. Was that what it was?"

"Those were letters," Clem said. "Folks loved letters back then."

"And after the war?" she asked, keeping it light, like she was asking about weather.

He finally looked at her, steady and unreadable. "After the war, it was different letters."

"Government letters?"

Clem gave a small shrug. "When Washington calls, some men pick up. That's all."

He wiped his hands, nodded at the pump. "Piston seal."

Then he added, casual as breath, "I figured you'd need one. I had an extra, so I brought it."

Millie shook her head, impressed in spite of herself. It wasn't magic, it was experience and blunt decisiveness.

"Ok, Mr. Fixit," she said, "can you do something about my uncle's truck? His tractor? The hole in the roof of the shed, and the holes in the roof of the house?"

Clem didn't even smile. He just looked past her shoulder at the shed roof, then at the porch boards, then at the truck sitting there, done for good.

"First thing, you eat," he said.

Millie blinked. "Excuse me?"

"You're shaking," Clem replied, like he was reading a gauge. "You've been hauling, yanking, and baking in the sun. You don't fix anything useful when you're half empty." He nodded toward the shack. "You got coffee in there? Anything?"

"I have pride," she said. "And a little food I saved from last night's dinner."

Clem's mouth flickered just enough to count as humor. "Pride won't hold a hammer."

Millie hated that she almost laughed.

He set his toolbox on the ground and started talking like the place already belonged to him. "After you eat, we handle the roof. We patch the worst holes first. Rain comes fast out here, and it doesn't care whose name is on the deed." He glanced at the sky like he'd scheduled the weather. "Then we check the fence line where that wire's cut. Then we see why your truck's dead. Tractor after that."

Millie planted her hands on her hips. "You're giving orders on my land."

Clem looked at her, steady and calm. "I'm giving priorities. If you want, we can spend the afternoon arguing about it. Or we can keep your roof from leaking on your bed."

There it was, the practical knife. No flourish. No pride. Just truth.

Millie felt relief loosen something in her chest, and irritation rushed in to cover it. She didn't like being relieved. She didn't like that her body trusted him, that the tight knot behind her ribs eased when he spoke like he knew what he was doing.

She forced her voice to stay sharp. "And you always talk like that?"

"Like what?"

"Like I'm one bad decision away from falling apart."

Clem picked up a board, tested it, then set it aside. "You're not falling apart," he said, softer. "You're getting introduced. The land does that. It tests you the first day so you'll respect it the second."

Millie swallowed. Gratitude tried to rise, unwanted and warm. She shoved it down, but it didn't go far.

"Fine," she said, too brisk. "A few bites since I have water now. Then roofs. Then fences. But you're not the boss of me."

Clem took a deep breath, like he'd accept any words that got her moving. "Good," he said. "Bosses get shot. Partners don't."

Millie heard it first. Tires on gravel, steady and sure. The gate chain clattered at the main entrance, the casual sound of a man who'd used that gate before.

Clem went still. Not tense, not afraid, just quiet in a way that made the air feel thinner.

"He's coming to make this your fault," Clem said, low. "Don't talk first. He'll try to make you apologize for standing on your own dirt." His eyes stayed on the fence line. "And don't explain. Explaining is a rope, they'll use it to pull you."

Millie's throat tightened. "Who is he?"

Clem didn't answer. He didn't have to.

A pickup rolled in, dark and clean for a ranch road. The driver climbed out like he'd done it a thousand times right here. It was Mr. Halverson. He wasn't just the man at the courthouse, his spread butted up against this place, and he knew exactly where fear lived. He carried entitlement like a birthright. He glanced at Millie, then at Clem, then back at Millie, as if Clem was a tool that came with the property.

"Well now," the man said, voice smooth. "I see the signs are back where they belong." He nodded toward the No Trespassing boards, like he'd personally approved their placement. "Water rights and lines don't always match the maps. Folks who understand that do fine."

Millie felt her cheeks heat. She opened her mouth.

Clem lifted a hand, small, firm. A translator's pause.

"What he means," Clem said, polite as Sunday, "is he's been treating your land like it's his, and he expected you to let him keep doing it."

Mr. Halverson's smile didn't move, but his eyes did. "Now, Clem, don't make it ugly. We're neighbors. We handle things reasonably."

Clem bit his lip. "Reasonable is fine," he said. "Start by unhooking your expectations from her property."

Millie felt the strange relief of being shielded, and it scared her more than the truck on the road. Clem had heard the song before, and he already knew how it ended.

Mr. Halverson stood by his open door like he was waiting for someone to apologize properly. The wind kept worrying the edges of his hat brim. His truck idled, patient and sure, like it had been invited.

Millie could feel the heat in her face again. She could feel the urge to explain, to defend, to speak first just to prove she could. Clem stayed beside her, quiet, watching Halverson the way a man watched a poker hand.

Halverson's smile held, smooth and practiced. "Now," he said, "we can do this neighborly, or we can do it the hard way."

Clem nodded. "Neighborly is fine," he said.

Before Millie could ask what he meant, Clem turned and started walking.

Halverson frowned. "Where you going?"

Clem didn't answer. He reached the nearest No Trespassing sign, the one tacked up like a warning and yanked it free. Nails squealed. The board popped loose. He carried it back without hurry. Then he went for the next one. And the next.

Millie watched, half stunned, half pleased, then immediately annoyed that she felt pleased. It was her land. She should be the one doing that. She also knew she didn't have the strength left in her arms to pull nails like that all day. Not after the pump, the stripped nut, the dry throat.

Halverson started forward. "You can't just take those."

Clem finally looked at him. His voice stayed calm. "You put them up. You can have them back."

He walked straight to Halverson's truck, stepped to the bed, and tossed the first sign in as if it were scrap lumber. Then another. The boards landed with flat, final thuds. Clem didn't stop. He loaded every sign he'd pulled, stacking them neat, almost polite.

Halverson's jaw worked. "What are you doing?"

Clem brushed sawdust off his hands. "Returning your signs. They don't belong on her property." He nodded toward the gate chain. "Put the chain back the way you found it, and drive out."

Halverson glanced at Millie, searching for her to take control back from Clem, searching for her to argue. Millie held still. She hated how protected she felt, and she hated how much she needed it.

Halverson's smile came back, thinner this time. "You're making this bigger than it needs to be."

Clem's answer was soft, almost friendly. "No, you made it bigger when you decided paperwork meant you could move people. Now you can go."

Halverson stared a moment longer, then climbed into his truck. The tires spit gravel when he left, like he wanted the land to remember him.

When the sound finally faded, Millie let out a breath she hadn't known she was holding. Relief came first. Then irritation followed, quick and sharp, because the relief felt like surrender.

Clem didn't watch the road. He watched her.

"This is survivable," he said. "But not by instinct. Not by pride. You need structure."

Millie lifted her chin. "I have structure."

Clem nodded, accepting the words the way he accepted daylight and dust. "Good. Then here's what it looks like."

He knelt by his toolbox and pulled out a worn folder, edges soft from use. He opened it like a man opening a map.

"I'll help you get fences tight, water steady, and supplies in. I'll introduce you to people who matter, the kind who don't smile at you like you're a mistake. I'll handle the neighbor pressure before it becomes a court date. If we need lumber, I'll get it. If we need a hand, I'll find one." He paused. "And you stop trying to do everything alone."

Millie wanted to argue. She wanted to say she didn't come here to be managed. But her shoulders ached. Her throat was still dry. The shack roof still had holes. The land still felt too big.

Clem added the part that shifted the room, even out here under open sky.

"Let me be the one who talks to them," he said. "Halverson, the bank, the feed store, the sheriff if it comes to that. You don't speak first. You don't explain. You let me do it."

Millie's eyes narrowed. "So I just stand there?"

"You stand there like the deed already knows your name," Clem said. "Because it does."

She didn't like how sensible it sounded. She didn't like how much she wanted to say yes.

Clem reached into the folder and pulled out a single sheet of paper, already typed, already neat. He had a pen, too.

"This is a simple agreement, similar to what you signed before, but more expansive." he said. "I'm not taking your land.

I'm not taking your say. I'm taking the paperwork heat. And working this land with you. You get help. I get authority to speak for you in limited places, sign for you, things like that so no one twists your words and makes you sign something foolish. This is the same kind of form you signed before," he said. "The limited one. This just finishes the filing side so nothing gets lost."

Millie stared at the page. She remembered the first form, the one he'd called specific and harmless, and she told herself this was just more of the same.

"You just carry that around?"

Clem's mouth barely smiled. "Standard."

"That's not an answer."

"It lets me speak for you when paper needs a mouth."

Millie didn't like how that sounded, but the water was running, and the day had already taught her what pride costs.

He tapped the paper. "You keep the land, Millie. I mean Mildred. I'll keep the paper from biting you."

He set the pen in her hand. Millie hesitated, the pen hovering over the blank line. She looked at Clem's unreadable face. He was a stranger who had shown up too perfectly, too prepared, with motives that felt wrapped in shadows. A smart woman would tell him to get off her land and never come back.

But a smart woman also knew how to read a calendar. She thought of the strict deadline Mrs. Raskin had hammered into her. She thought of her uncle's fragile claim, the empty bank account, and the terrifying reality of Halverson's smile. She was completely out of time, out of money, and out of options. She was not trusting Clem because she was naive. She was using his labor and his knowledge because she was desperate.

She signed the paper, not out of blind faith, but because it was the only weapon she had left. Halverson's truck had just driven off with his No Trespassing signs in his bed instead of staked across her land, and she needed Clem to keep it that way.

Clem folded the paper and slid it into his folder. Then he tore off a carbon copy and handed it to her as if it were a consolation prize.

"You keep the copy," he said. "I'll keep the original. It's safer with me."

Millie held the thin sheet and felt relief settle in her bones, wearing the disguise of surrender.

CHAPTER FIVE

THE WITNESSES

Millie kept the copy folded tight in her pocket like it might blow away if she breathed wrong. Every time she moved, she felt the thin paper shift, a reminder that the original was somewhere else, in Clem's folder. She told herself it didn't matter. The water was running, and the day had stopped trying to kill her.

That evening they worked shoulder to shoulder until the light went soft and the wind cooled down. Clem didn't talk much, he just moved from problem to problem like he'd been born with a checklist.

By sundown, her uncle's truck turned over like it had been waiting on the right hands.

Millie leaned against the fender, grinning in spite of herself. "Well," she said, "now it's my truck."

Clem shut the hood and wiped his hands on a rag. "That's the idea."

The tractor started next, a steady rumble that sounded almost pleased. The shed roof got patched, and Clem tapped the board once like a judge calling it settled. "No more rain coming in there."

The house's roof was the last surprise. Millie had expected disaster, but it was mostly a loose shingle and a stubborn nail. When it finally sat right, she let out a laugh that felt brand new.

"That means I'm sleeping here tonight," she said. "On my land."

Clem nodded. His eyes stayed serious. "Tomorrow, we find a witness to sign that affidavit. No," he corrected himself, "we find two witnesses. That way we stay ahead of the contest Halverson's going to file."

Millie watched him think. You could almost see the boxes being checked behind his eyes.

"Luckily your uncle worked this land just over five years before he had to leave," Clem said. "You've got the deep well, a residence, a shed. That matters."

Millie wiped a smear of dust off her wrist. "But what about the cultivating clause? I know he tried corn, wheat, even soybeans. All that's dead and long gone."

Clem didn't miss a beat. "He also planted crested wheatgrass. East pasture. Plenty of it. That qualifies."

Millie frowned. "How do you know all that? Proving up, cultivation, what counts, what doesn't."

Clem answered too fast, like the words slipped off the edge of his thoughts. "Because your file said you'd try to do it the hard way."

Millie went still. "My file?"

A pause, small but real.

"Your paperwork," he corrected. "County offices keep notes. Men like Halverson keep notes too." He tipped his head toward the darkening road. "This place runs on notes."

Millie didn't love it, but it fit the day she'd just lived. She swallowed it down and told herself what she wanted to believe. He wasn't a bad man.

Clem snapped the toolbox shut, changing the subject before

her mind could pick at it. "While I'm lining up witnesses, you take that rental truck back into town."

Millie narrowed her eyes. "And make sure I don't pay for it again, since I paid for the blown tire."

Clem nodded. "Also tell him he needs to return the rim, or Earl's going to charge him for it."

She lifted her chin. "Meet you at the diner?"

"Ten sharp," Clem said. "We'll ride back in my truck. After that, you keep yours."

* * *

MILLIE SLEPT hard in the house. Not comfortable, not fancy, but safe enough. When morning came, she woke with a strange feeling. Hope, with a bruise on it. This was only her third day in Montana, but it felt like a lifetime.

Returning the rental truck went smoother than it should've. The man at the lot tried to push her around, tried to talk in circles like she was supposed to get confused and apologize. Millie raised her voice, stomped her foot once, and watched him blink like he hadn't expected resistance to come in a skirt.

She walked away before he could find his footing.

She reached the diner twenty minutes early. The bell over the door jingled, bright and familiar. Doris looked up, wiped her hands on her apron, and smiled like she'd been waiting.

"Well, let me impress you, Ms. Mildred," Doris said. "How's your business going?"

Millie paused. Doris remembered her name, remembered she mattered. The diner wasn't just a place to eat, it was a place where news sat down at the counter and ordered coffee.

Doris poured her a cup without asking. "Just in case you forgot, I'm Doris, and breakfast is outstanding. What you'll have?"

Millie smiled. "I'll take whatever you got."

"I'll get right on it."

As Doris walked away, a man came in from the direction of the feed store and slid onto a stool at the counter without looking around. He had a sharp way about him, like he enjoyed trouble because it made him feel important.

Millie leaned toward Doris when she returned. "What's his name?"

"Wade," Doris murmured. "He's big trouble. You'd do best to stay away."

At ten o'clock sharp, Clem walked in. He didn't scan the room like a nervous man, but he saw everything anyway. As Clem sat down, Wade clicked his heel against the stool rung, a little noise like a signal.

A second later, Clem did the same thing, heel to rung, one clean click.

Millie noticed. It felt odd. Then she told herself it was nothing and pushed the thought aside.

On the drive back, Clem kept his eyes on the road and his voice on the work.

"I've got two witnesses lined up," he said. "I filed a few papers to shore up…" He hesitated, almost said his claim, then corrected without a stumble. "…your claim. All we got left is to sign some papers at the county office with the witnesses."

Millie stared out at the land rolling toward them, wide and dry and waiting. She didn't think he noticed how her fingers tightened around the edge of her purse.

They pulled up near the house. Before either of them got out, Clem reached over and took her hand. It wasn't rough. It wasn't urgent. It was steady, like he was trying to anchor her.

"Day before yesterday you said 'we'," Clem said. "Did you mean that like a boss, or a partner?"

Millie blinked. "I don't even remember saying it."

"You did."

She thought for a beat. "I don't know. I guess I gotta think about that."

Clem nodded. "Fair enough. Time's critical. According to the county office, we've got less than a week to nail down the witnesses and file it right." He emphasized we, just slightly. "After that, we wait. With your uncle's history, what he built, what he proved, the land ought to be yours. Private property."

Millie couldn't help noticing his hand around hers. Soft, careful, kind. Not the Clem she met two days ago. She noticed other things too, the blue in his eyes, the tone of that rough voice when it gentled, even the clean smell of soap and dust.

All she managed, before she opened the door and stepped back onto her land, was one quiet word.

"Ok."

* * *

ON ONLY HER fourth day in Montana, Millie woke at five with the strange feeling that she belonged to something. The house was still a shack, the boards still creaked, and dust still lived in the corners like it had nowhere better to be. But the pump worked. The roof didn't leak. The truck started. And the land, for the first time since she'd stepped off that bus, felt quiet instead of hostile.

She had found coffee beans and a grinder in her uncle's cabinet, as well as a solid brick of old sugar. She made a strong pot that brewed up slowly. She poured coffee and stepped outside with the cup warming her hands. The sky was pale, the air cool, and the pasture lay out there wide and patient. Millie breathed in slow, then let it out even slower. She could breathe. She could see the work ahead without it looking impossible.

Back inside, she started cleaning with purpose. Sweeping. Mopping. Straightening. Fixing what she could, setting piles for what she couldn't. Confidence wasn't something you found, it was something you built one small task at a time.

She stopped near the table and prayed out loud, because the silence felt too big. She thanked the Lord for the land, for her uncle, and for Clem. She thanked Him for a man who showed up when she was thirsty, tired, and one stripped nut away from quitting. Then she made a decision. When Clem came back today, she'd tell him that "we" meant partners.

Clem didn't roll in until eleven. Late, for him.

Millie saw the red truck through the window and touched her chest like she was checking if her heart was still there. It was. It was loud about it too.

He climbed out carrying that worn folder. The same folder that had been in her hands when she arrived. Now it was in his hands, casual, like the paper belonged to him.

Clem walked up the steps and knocked. When Millie opened the door, her smile came fast and bright.

"Partner," she said, and the word surprised even her. "And you can call me Millie."

Clem held still for a half second. The smile. The trust. The way she said it like tomorrow was certain. Something shifted behind his eyes, quick and quiet, like a crack in glass you didn't see until the light hit it.

He cleared his throat. "We've got to go to town. Right now. Witnesses are meeting us at the diner, then we'll head to the county office to sign papers."

Millie nodded, already moving. "Then let's go. Your truck or mine?"

Clem took a deep breath, like he was bracing for something. "Mine."

* * *

THE DINER BELL jingled when they walked in. Doris looked up and greeted them like they'd been doing this for years.

"Millie. Clem."

Coffee arrived as if it were part of the furniture. Millie sat there with her hands around the cup, warm and steady, and thought, just for a moment, that maybe this could be her life. Work. Land. Coffee. And a man who knew the rules.

Clem leaned back slightly. "Doris," he said, "who's working the county window today?"

Doris smiled like she'd heard the question in her sleep. "Oh, Clem. Why do we do this dance? You know and I'm not saying."

Millie noticed something then. Clem smiled. Not much, but it was there. It made him look younger, and it made Millie feel foolish for noticing.

The bell jingled again.

Two men walked in. Doris said their names without warmth. "Wade. Brooks." Then she rolled her eyes like she wanted the floor to open up and take them.

Wade slid onto the bench with a confidence that didn't belong to him. Brooks followed, quieter, watching everything.

Clem didn't waste time. "They're the witnesses," he said to Millie. "Two signatures. That's what we need."

Millie's stomach tightened. "I don't know these men."

Before Clem could answer, Wade smiled, shifty and eager. "Oh yes, ma'am. This kind of thing is done all the time 'round here."

Millie's gut said stop. Doris's face said stop too, every time Millie looked her way. But Clem was already standing, already moving the day forward like it had wheels and he had his foot on the gas.

"Let's go," Clem said. "County office."

As they walked into the courthouse, Clem peeled off. "I've got to handle one thing," he said. "One minute."

He disappeared down the hall.

Less than a minute later they were standing at the county window. Mrs. Raskin looked exactly like she had before, as if her face had been stamped onto her head and sealed there.

Millie expected ceremony. She expected a speech. She expected something that felt like winning. Instead, it was simple.

Sign here. Initial here. Do you have this? Do you have that?

File. Close. Done.

Mrs. Raskin said, "I want to make you aware that Mr. Halverson filed a contest. This will be considered. The final decision rests with the land office commissioner. Your paperwork is in order and filed properly, that is in your favor. The commissioner will visit next week. If everything checks out, he'll make a decision and likely issue final certification as soon as the government allows."

Relief washed through Millie so hard her knees went loose. She'd done it. She'd gotten ahead of the trap. She'd survived the first round.

Then she saw Wade's face.

Satisfaction, quick and ugly.

Wade and Brooks shook hands like they'd just won something. Then they turned to Clem and held out their hands, both of them.

Clem didn't move.

His eyes went to Millie, and something lived there that Millie had not seen before.

Dread.

Like a man caught mid-act, hand deep in a cookie jar, trying to decide whether to run or tell the truth.

Clem's voice stayed soft. "Millie, can you come with me please?"

Millie followed him down the hall, the same direction he'd slipped off to before. They stopped outside a door with a nameplate.

Judge Harlan B. Whitaker.

Clem took a breath, then looked at her like the next sentence could change both of their lives.

"Do you trust me?" he asked.

Millie swallowed. "Yes, but you're making me nervous."

Clem voice was rough. "I did a bad thing. I can't get out of it clean. But I can fix it. This is the only way."

He took both her hands. His grip was steady, his eyes serious, his voice almost quiet enough to be mistaken for prayer.

"Will you marry me?"

Then he knocked on the judge's door.

Millie stood there, mouth open, heart pounding, relief and fear wrestling in her ribs. She stared at him, searching for the man who fixed her pump, her roof, her hope.

"Say it plain," she whispered. "What happens if I say no?"

Clem's face went still. No charm. No dodging. Just the truth settling in.

"If you say no," he said, "you lose everything."

Millie blinked. "Everything?"

"Your place," Clem said. "Your chance to keep it. Those two behind us will take it, and I won't be able to stop it." He swallowed once, and his voice dropped. "And if you don't marry me, then I'm the one who ends up holding the paper. Not because I want to own you, but because that's how this ugly thing is set up."

Millie stared at him, breath shallow. "So this is my only way out."

"It's the only way I can fix what I broke," he said. "And it's the only way you don't get wiped out."

The hall felt smaller. The courthouse felt like a trap.

"Clem," she whispered, "are we partners, or are you the boss?"

His answer came fast.

"Partners," he said. "Definitely."

Millie's breath caught.

"Ok," she said, and she didn't know if it was surrender or faith.

"Partners."

CHAPTER SIX

MAN AND WIFE

The hallway smelled like floor wax and old paper. The judge's door had a frosted window and a brass knob worn smooth by other people's urgency. Clem pushed in without waiting for permission, Millie half a step behind.

The judge stood behind a scarred desk with his coat off, sleeves rolled, like he'd been interrupted in the middle of something that mattered more than this.

He didn't bother with a smile. "Clem, we're in a big hurry."

Clem glanced at Millie, then back at the judge. "We're ready."

Millie stayed near the doorway for a second. The room was small and plain. Two chairs. A flag in the corner. A clock that ticked too loud. On the wall, a framed certificate that looked older than both of them.

Two courthouse staff sat along the side wall, pulled in to witness. They held pens like they'd signed a hundred lives into place and would sign a hundred more before lunch.

The judge cleared his throat and picked up the first page. "Clement Spyker. Do you take Mildred Caldwell to be your lawful wife?"

Clem didn't hesitate. "I do." He pulled a ring from his pocket and gave it to Millie.

Millie watched his mouth form the words. Easy. Clean. Like he'd said them before.

The judge turned to her. "Mildred Caldwell. Do you take Clement Spyker to be your lawful husband?"

For half a breath, Millie felt the room tilt. She'd imagined marriage once, back when she still imagined things. A church. Flowers. Someone's hand squeezing hers because he meant it. Not this. Not a courthouse office with a tired clock and strangers holding clipboards.

This felt like buying a car. Sign here. Initial there. Drive it home and hope it runs.

But she felt the ring in her hand. It was real, and the man standing beside her was real too. He'd fixed her pump. He'd patched her roof. He'd walked her right up to this door and asked the question that changed everything.

Hope with sharp edges, she thought. The kind that cuts if you grip it wrong.

"I do," she said, and with quivering hands, she slipped the ring on her finger.

The judge didn't react. He slid the paper forward. "Sign here. Both of you."

Millie took the pen. The paper had a rough tooth to it, and the ink smelled sharp, like metal. She wrote her name slowly, neatly, the way her mother had taught her. Her nervous hand had calmed enough to sign, even if her stomach hadn't.

Clem signed next. His name moved fast across the line, confident and practiced. Millie noticed that too, and it sat in her chest like a pebble she couldn't swallow.

The witnesses stood, one at a time, and signed without looking up. The clerk stamped the page hard enough to make the desk jump.

The judge gathered the papers, stacked them, and spoke again. "By the authority vested in me, I pronounce you man and wife."

Man and wife.

No pause for the words to settle. No room for romance. Still, the sentence landed like a gate slamming shut behind them.

Millie's throat went tight. Clem's jaw flexed once. He stared straight ahead, but his eyes looked farther than the wall.

The judge nodded toward the door. "That's it. You're done."

Done.

They turned to leave. Millie felt like she'd crossed a line she couldn't step back over, and the strange part was she'd chosen it. She'd said yes. She'd signed her name. She'd done it with her eyes open.

In the hallway, Clem slowed. He shifted his hat, then offered his arm, formal as Sunday and careful as a man approaching a skittish horse.

Millie didn't take it.

She didn't step away either.

They stood close enough that the warmth of his sleeve brushed her coat. Millie took one breath, then another. The only thing she could remember, clear as a photograph, was the smell of that paper.

Clem looked down at her. "You alright?"

Millie heard her own voice before she felt it. "No."

He nodded once, like he understood and didn't plan to argue. "We'll be alright anyway."

Millie stared at the closed door behind them, then at the long hallway ahead.

Partners, she reminded herself. Partners, even if it hurt.

"Let's go," she said.

And together, they walked out of the courthouse.

* * *

CLEM'S TRUCK rolled out of town like it couldn't wait to forget the courthouse. Gravel popped under the tires. The sky was the same wide gray it had been all morning, and the land opened up around them, flat and honest and too big to hide in.

Millie sat stiff in the passenger seat, hands folded in her lap like she was holding herself together. The ring felt heavier now, like it had weight beyond metal. She looked at it for the first time. A thin silver band, a small turquoise stone. Simple. Practical.

They drove in silence long enough for the courthouse to shrink in the rearview mirror. Long enough for Millie to hear every rattle in the dash, every breath Clem took.

The road cut past the first cattle ranch, a long fence line and black shapes moving slow in winter grass. Twenty minutes in, Clem cleared his throat like the sound might make this easier.

"I guess I owe you an explanation."

Millie didn't look at him. She kept her eyes forward, fixed on the road like it could tell her what to do next. "You do."

Clem nodded like he deserved the cold in her voice. He kept both hands on the wheel.

"I didn't come to your place by accident," he said. "I heard you were alone. Heard you were holding on by your fingernails."

Millie clenched her jaw. She watched a hawk ride the wind over the ditch line. "From who?"

"Doesn't matter," Clem said. "What matters is I knew Wade and Brooks were sniffing around, and I knew they'd get to you sooner or later."

Millie finally turned her head, not all the way, just enough to see the side of his face. "So you got to me first."

"Yes."

The truth was clean. No excuses. No softening. That almost made it worse.

Clem kept talking. "They want that stretch of land to connect their holdings. Water. Grazing rights. Control. If they get it, they squeeze anyone near them until there's nothing left but what they own."

Millie stared out the window. The cows looked peaceful, heads down, chewing like the world had never broken anyone's heart.

She swallowed hard. She wasn't going to cry. Not in front of him. Not today. She'd been in Montana less than a week. She'd been tired, desperate, hopeful, and now she was married.

Swindled, a part of her whispered.

Or saved, another part argued.

Millie didn't know which voice to trust.

Clem's voice stayed steady, quieter than it had been in the judge's office. "I fixed the pump because you needed it fixed. I patched your roof because it was the right thing. But I also did it because I wanted you to rely on me."

Millie's fingers curled tight. "So that I'd say yes."

"So that you'd trust me," he said. "Yes."

Silence filled the cab again. The heater hummed. The tires sang on the road. Millie turned fully toward the window and watched the grass blur by, the fence posts ticking past like a slow-counting clock.

Clem took a breath that sounded like it hurt. "I'm not going to lecture you. I'm not going to pretend I was noble. I did what I did because I wanted the outcome."

Millie's voice came out thin. "My land."

"Our land," Clem said, then stopped himself, like the word didn't belong in his mouth yet. "It was your land. And they were coming for it."

Millie looked down at her hands. She technically still owned it, at least in her mind. She needed that thought, even if it was just a plank in deep water.

Clem stared at the road. "I'm telling you now because we can't build anything on lies. Not after today."

Millie let out a breath. "We already did."

Clem flinched, just a small movement in his jaw. "Yes."

Another mile passed. Then he said, "I won't hide anything from you again. I won't take from you, not money, not papers, not decisions. I won't deceive you, not once."

Millie's heart thumped hard. Vows, she thought. A day late.

Clem's grip tightened on the wheel. "And I will protect... this place." He paused, and for a second he sounded like a man choosing his words with both hands. "My land, no. It's not mine. It's ours. I'll protect it with my life if it comes to that."

Millie turned from the window, eyes sharp now. "Don't say it like that."

"Like what?"

"Like you can make it all right with a promise," she said. "I don't know what you are, Clem. I don't know what part of you is real."

He glanced at her, then back to the road. "All of me is real. Some of it is ugly."

Millie's throat constricted. Fear lived right under her skin, bright and ready. "Are we partners?" she asked again. "Together?"

Clem answered fast, like he'd been waiting for the question. "Yes. For sure, partners."

Millie studied him. He didn't smile. He didn't charm. He just held the road like it mattered.

Clem swallowed once. "I married you to keep you safe," he said. Then his voice dropped, rougher. "And somewhere between your pump and your roof and you standing there not quitting, I fell in love with you."

The words hit tender and terrible at the same time.

She looked back out at the land and felt hope rise, sharp-edged, cutting on the way up. She didn't answer him yet, but she didn't tell him to stop either.

* * *

That night, all things considered, Clem decided sleeping at Millie's house was out of the question.

He stood on her porch under a weak porch light, hat in his hands. Millie didn't ask him to stay. She didn't ask him to leave either. She just watched him with that new look, the one that said she was measuring the damage and the man who caused it.

Clem gave a short nod. "I'll be back in the morning."

Millie's mouth tightened, like she might say something sharp, or something that hurt more because it was true. She didn't say anything.

Clem walked away and felt the word honeymoon float through his head like a bad joke.

His place in town was small, quiet, and too clean. He slept light, woke before dawn, and by habit more than hunger, he stopped at the diner.

The bell over the door jingled. Doris was behind the counter, and Clem knew the moment she saw him. Her shoulders went stiff. Her eyes did that quick up and down, the kind women use when they're deciding if a man deserves another inch of kindness.

Clem slid onto his usual stool.

Doris didn't move.

No smile. No "Morning, Clem." No coffee appearing like it always had.

When she finally poured it, she set the mug down with a thud that made the spoon jump. "There," she said, flat.

Clem looked at her. "Morning, Doris."

She stared back. "Don't 'morning' me."

Clem didn't argue. He took a slow sip like he had all day.

The door jingled again. Wade and Brooks walked in, loud boots, loud voices, acting like the diner belonged to them. Doris didn't greet them either. She turned away like she'd found something important to clean.

Wade saw Clem and smiled. Brooks followed, grin sharp and friendly in the way a knife can be friendly.

They didn't ask. They sat down at Clem's table.

Brooks leaned in. "Well, would you look at that. Married man."

Wade's eyes were bloodshot, his smile ugly. "You think you're clever."

Clem kept his coffee in both hands. "I think you're late."

Brooks chuckled. "We're gonna expose what you did."

Wade slammed his palm on the table, not hard enough to spill the coffee, but hard enough to make a point. "Give us our cut."

Clem's face didn't move. "There is no cut."

Brooks lowered his voice. "Your wife is in danger. She can be run off. Accidents happen."

Clem's eyes stayed calm, but the air around him went colder. He set his mug down, slow. "Listen close."

Wade smirked. Clem didn't.

"I have witnesses," Clem said. "I have papers, dates, signatures, filed in the courthouse. You have nothing but a bad attitude and a reputation."

Brooks' smile thinned. "Reputation doesn't stop a man."

"It does when the sheriff already knows your names," Clem said. "I told him everything. Not because I'm scared, but because I'm done playing."

Wade's eyes flicked, just once, toward the windows. The street outside. The morning traffic.

Clem leaned back. "If anything happens to Millie, I hand over the whole folder. Every detail. And the law won't have to guess who to look at first."

Brooks sat up straighter. Wade's jaw worked.

Clem stood. "It's over."

He slid a bill under his mug, then paused, looking at them both. "I fell in love," he said. "And that's that."

Wade didn't speak. Brooks didn't either.

Clem turned toward the counter. Doris was watching him like she didn't want to.

"Morning, Doris," Clem said again, quieter.

Then he walked out and headed for the land.

Clem pulled up slow, dust curling behind the tires. Millie was out by the fence, standing still, staring across the land like she was trying to memorize it before someone took it away.

He got out and started toward her, careful with his steps, careful with his breathing.

Millie lifted her hand, palm out, like a traffic cop.

Clem stopped dead.

For a second, the only sound was wind in dry grass and the faint creak of an old gate.

Millie didn't turn around. "Why are you here?"

Clem swallowed. "Because we've got work to do before the land office commissioner shows up."

Millie's shoulders didn't soften. "Work?"

"Yes," Clem said, quick, then steadier. "Fence line. Livestock. A shed for supplies. Things that need doing."

Millie finally turned, and the look on her face stopped him harder than her hand ever could.

She stepped closer, just enough to make the air between them feel tight. "You said you fell in love."

Clem nodded, once.

Millie's voice stayed level, but it cut. "Do you love me, Clem, or did you fall in love with the land, so you stole it?"

Clem's shoulders sagged like he'd been holding them up with stubbornness alone. He dropped his eyes for a moment, then forced them back up.

"I'm sorry," he said. "I told you I'd never lie to you again." His mouth worked like the truth had edges. "The honest answer is both."

Millie held his gaze. "Both?"

Clem nodded again. "Both."

She studied him like she'd studied broken boards and bad weather, trying to figure out what was solid and what would give way.

"So, you do love me?" she said.

"Yes."

"In less than a week," Millie said, disbelief and fear braided together. "You know that for sure."

Clem's voice got rough, not angry, just scraped raw. "I had girlfriends after the war. Not many. None of it stuck." He looked away, then back, like it hurt to be seen. "Nobody ever touched me deep down the way you did. The way you didn't quit, even when you had every reason to. I saw that and it got inside me."

Millie took one more step. Close now. Close enough to smell the cold on his coat.

She looked him straight in the eyes and felt something she hated how much she wanted, honesty.

Millie kissed him.

It was fast, more decision than romance, but it was a kiss. Clem froze like his body didn't know what to do with kindness.

Millie pulled back first. She didn't smile, not yet, but her eyes softened a fraction. "You start that work," she said. "I'll make lunch."

Clem blinked once, then nodded. "Alright."

He walked off toward the fence line, and Millie went inside like a new wife in a strange kitchen, trying too hard not to look like she didn't belong.

She found bread, a pan, a bit of bacon. Simple food. Practical food. The kind she could control.

Then she tried to do one thing extra, because she wanted today to feel like a start.

That's when the smoke started.

The pan went too hot. The bacon burned fast, black at the edges, and the small house filled up like a chimney. Millie yanked the pan off, coughing, waving a dish towel like it could fight smoke.

The front door opened.

Clem stepped in and stopped, taking in the haze, the smell, Millie's red face, her hair half loose like she'd wrestled the stove and lost.

Millie's stomach dropped. "I... I ruined it."

Clem's mouth curved, that small smile she'd seen in the diner, the one that wasn't mocking, just amused at life's timing.

Millie had liked it then. She liked it now, maybe more.

Clem didn't scold. He walked to the window, shoved it up, then opened the back door. The wind pulled the smoke out in long gray ribbons.

He took the pan, scraped off the worst, and set it aside as if it wasn't the end of the world. "We'll eat," he said. "Just not fancy."

They sat at the table with bread and what was salvageable of the bacon. Millie kept her eyes on her plate, embarrassed.

Clem ate like a man who'd had worse and lived.

After a few bites, he said, "You worried about Wade and Brooks?"

Millie looked up. "I'm worried about everything."

Clem nodded like that was fair. "I saw them this morning."

Millie's spine stiffened. "And?"

"And they tried," he said. "They sat at my table. They threatened. They wanted a cut." He met her eyes. "I told them it's over. I told them I've got witnesses and papers and that the sheriff already knows."

Millie stared at him. "You told the sheriff."

"I did."

Something moved in Millie's chest, part relief, part fear. Clem was capable, and that was comforting, but also terrifying.

She set her hands on the table, steadying herself. "You're... great," she said, then shook her head like she didn't trust the word. "And you're scary."

Clem's expression didn't change much, but his eyes did. "I'm trying to be better than what I've been."

Millie nodded slowly. Then, almost at the same time, they both said it.

"We're married."

Millie's mouth curved first, small and surprised.

Clem's smile followed, just as slight.

It wasn't a honeymoon.

But it felt like a start.

* * *

THAT EVENING, after the dishes and the quiet, Clem stood by the door like a man waiting for permission he didn't deserve.

"I'll head back to town," he said. "To my place."

Millie frowned. "But aren't you already home?"

The question hit him in the chest. Clem blinked like he hadn't heard her right.

Millie stepped closer, reached for his hand. He hesitated, then took hers, rough palm against rough palm. Her grip was steady, like she'd decided something.

Clem's voice came low. "Millie…"

She rose onto her toes and kissed him.

This time it wasn't a quick decision. It was a choice. Slow, certain, and close enough to make both of them forget the courthouse for a minute.

Clem didn't pull away. He leaned in like he'd been waiting for that permission all day.

Later, when the lamp was out and the house settled, they ended up in the same bed for the first time. Millie's bed. Millie's room. The place she'd called hers, even when nothing felt like it belonged to her anymore.

Morning came early. The light was pale and thin. Millie woke with Clem beside her and for one startled second, she forgot everything that led them here.

Then she remembered, and she didn't move away.

Clem's hand rested on the quilt between them, not demanding, just there. Millie watched his breathing, the way his face looked softer in sleep, like the hard parts took a rest when nobody was watching.

He opened his eyes. "Morning."

Millie swallowed. "Morning."

They lay still a moment, then reality came back in a list. Fence. Feed. Repairs. Work that didn't care how tired you were.

Clem pushed up, stretched, and said, "Chores."

Millie gave a short laugh. "I didn't understand that word until I got here."

Clem's mouth flickered. "Most folks don't."

By midmorning they were out at the barn. That's what Clem called it. Millie still wanted to call it a mess of boards with a roof that looked tired.

The tractor sat inside, half-shadowed. Millie followed Clem's directions, trying hard to be useful and not in the way.

Her eyes caught a post near the tractor, slightly crooked, like it had been shoved there for no reason. It looked temporary, like someone had braced something and forgot to take it out.

Millie pointed. "What's this doing here?"

Clem was on the other side, digging through tools. "Leave it."

Millie heard him, but she didn't understand why. The post looked like clutter. And clutter, she thought, was the enemy of getting things done.

She stepped toward it. "It's in the way."

"Millie," Clem said, sharper.

Too late.

Millie grabbed the post and shoved. It gave easier than she expected, and the instant it moved, the roof answered.

A crack, a groan, then a hard snap that turned her blood cold.

The corner of the roof dropped. Boards split. Dust burst down. Millie threw her arms up and stumbled back.

Something slammed onto the tractor with a sound like thunder. A smaller piece clipped her forearm, scraping skin. It didn't hurt much, but the fear hit like a hammer.

Millie froze, chest heaving, staring at what she'd done.

If the tractor hadn't been there, if it hadn't taken the weight, she knew exactly where that roof would've landed.

On her.

Clem was beside her in two strides. He grabbed her shoulders, turned her slightly, eyes scanning fast. "Are you OK?"

Millie blinked. "I... I think so."

He lifted her arm, checked the scrape. A thin line of blood. Nothing deep. Clem's breath eased out.

"That's all that matters," he said, voice soft now. "You hear me? You matter more than any roof."

Millie swallowed hard. Pride burned hotter than the scrape. "I messed up. I knocked it down."

Clem looked at the fallen corner, the broken boards, the dust settling like shame. He didn't curse. He didn't throw his hat. He didn't even raise his voice. "That post was holding rot together. You couldn't see it."

Millie's eyes stung. "It's going to cost money we don't have."

Clem's gaze moved back to her. "We'll figure it out."

Millie took a step toward the ladder. "I can fix it. I can get up there right now."

Clem caught her wrist, firm but gentle. "Not yet. First rule, you don't climb when you're shook up."

Millie opened her mouth.

Clem added, "Second rule, you don't climb without knowing where the weak spots are."

That stopped her. Clem pointed out the beam, the rot line, the way the roof had been relying on one last stubborn piece of wood. He didn't lecture, but he did teach, plain and steady.

Then he put her to work.

"Hand me boards," he said. "And clear debris away from the tractor."

Millie did it fast, determined. She hauled broken pieces out, stacked usable boards, swept dust, and kept her eyes on Clem's hands as he nailed fresh supports into place.

They worked side by side all day. No speeches. Just effort.

By evening, the barn still looked rough, but it wasn't falling anymore. The tractor was safe. Clem had braced the opening with fresh timber.

Millie wiped her forehead with her sleeve and looked at Clem. "I'm sorry."

Clem shook his head once. "You didn't quit."

Millie's throat went tight. She nodded.

Hope with sharp edges, she thought again.

But tonight, it felt like they'd earned a little of it.

* * *

IT HAD BEEN a little over two months since Millie stepped off the bus and tried to look like she belonged.

The troubles she'd feared most never came. Doris told her the sheriff had paid Wade and Brooks a visit, then the two of them left town like men who suddenly remembered they had somewhere else to be. Millie didn't celebrate, not out loud anyway. She just let herself breathe again.

That morning, she stood at the stove, bacon popping, coffee strong, eggs going in the pan. The kitchen had started to feel lived-in. Not pretty, not easy, but theirs.

* * *

CLEM SAT AT THE TABLE, watching her. He didn't say much. He just watched the way she moved, sure now, like work had stitched itself into her bones. He thought about the last few weeks, how fast everything had turned, and how close he'd come to wrecking the best thing he'd ever touched.

He was proud, too. Proud he'd beaten Wade and Brooks. Proud he'd won.

Then the shame would rise, quiet and steady, because winning had started as a con.

He looked past Millie, out the window at the fence line and the fields, and the old thought came easy.

My land.

Clem's jaw shifted once. He corrected it in his head like a man correcting himself in church.

Our land. Millie's too.

* * *

MILLIE CARRIED his plate to the table. She set down the eggs and coffee, then paused. The smell hit her wrong, sharp and heavy, like it had claws.

Her hand flew to her mouth.

She swallowed hard, eyes wide, and bolted for the door.

Clem was up before the chair stopped moving.

Outside, Millie bent over and vomited hard into the dirt. When it eased, she stayed there, breathing fast, staring at the ground like it might give her an answer.

But she already had one.

Times. Weeks. The way her body had felt. The eggs turning her stomach for days. It all snapped into place.

She'd thought she was scared before.

Now she was terrified.

Clem stepped close, careful, and rested his hand on her shoulder. "You ok?"

Millie wiped her mouth with the back of her hand. "Yes."

But the way she said it told him everything.

Clem's fingers pressed once, gentle. "All three of us," he said, voice low, steady, "we'll make it work."

Millie let out a shaky breath that was almost a laugh, almost a sob.

She smiled at him.

Then she vomited again.

CHAPTER SEVEN

NEAR THE RIDGE

*O*nly a month into Millie's sickness, the knock came like a wrong note in a hymn.

Nobody visited this far out. Not unless something was on fire, or somebody was dead.

Clem opened the door and found a postman in a dust-coated hat, shifting his weight uncomfortably.

"Mister Spyker?" he asked.

Clem nodded.

"Registered letter from the county office."

Clem signed, and the man watched him do it, careful as if the ink mattered more than the name. When the postman left, the still rushed back in. Clem tore the envelope open at the table.

Land Commissioner. Inspection. Less than a week.

The paper slid from Clem's fingers and landed flat.

Millie leaned over it, one hand pressed to her middle. Her face went pale, then green.

"Don't," Clem said, already moving.

"I'm fine," she lied, then hurried outside, retching into the grass.

When she came back in, wiping her mouth with her sleeve,

Clem had the tools out and started naming things out loud, fence line, water barrel, the lean-to, the yard, the stove pipe. And a few more things that looked like neglect. Millie joined him between waves of nausea, hauling, scrubbing, and straightening. Clem tried to keep her on light work, but she kept showing up anyway. She had that look, the one that said she was done being carried.

By the time the commissioner arrived, the place looked like a ranch that was meant to last. The man walked slowly, clipboard tucked to his chest, boots clean enough to shame the porch. He asked almost nothing. He looked, measured, and checked boxes quietly with a pencil that never hesitated.

Then he paused and glanced up. "How long have you been on the property?"

"Several months now," Clem said.

The commissioner nodded once and went back to the page. "You did good."

Clem looked like he'd been bracing for suspicion, not praise.

He kept moving, kept checking. Check. Check. Check. Clem watched every mark as if it were a verdict, and when the man finally looked up again, Clem couldn't help it, he smiled.

*　*　*

NOT LONG AFTER, Clem and Millie went into town in stiff clothes and dusty boots. Uneasy nerves. The county office smelled like it always did, ink and old paper. The permit was granted, signed, stamped, official. Even Halverson went quiet after that. Once the county stamped the paper, he knew the law was on the Spyker's side, and men like him didn't fight battles they couldn't win on paper.

Clem tried to play it cool, but his hands gave him away when he touched that paper. Millie felt the floor steady under her, for the first time since she stepped off that bus.

Then the county clerk, Mrs. Raskin, cleared her throat.

"There are conditions. Follow-up inspections. Improvements must continue."

Millie's smile stayed in place, but her grip tightened. This wasn't a gift. It was a leash.

On the ride back, she held the permit like fragile glass. Clem drove like he was hauling gold.

Millie's sickness didn't fade. It settled into a daily routine. Dawn, midday, sometimes right after she'd sworn she was past it. She learned that plain crackers and water would settle her stomach. This was the new normal, and nobody had asked her permission.

Clem finally insisted they go to the doctor in town. The little office smelled like antiseptic, with a calendar on the wall that was already out of date. The doctor didn't waste time or comfort.

"Yep," he said, looking over his notes. "You're pregnant."

Millie suspected it, but her joy came first, fast and bright, like a match struck in a dark room. She pressed a hand to her belly and almost laughed. Then fear punched in right behind it, hard enough to steal her breath.

Money. Food. Warmth. Being pregnant in the middle of the winter everybody talked about was difficult. The cold didn't just chill you, it tried to take you.

Outside, the wind cut across the street, and Millie pulled her coat tight. Clem stood close, one hand hovering at her elbow like he could shield her from the weather and the whole world at once. His face didn't change much, but his eyes did. Protective. Focused. Controlled, like he was afraid emotion would jinx it.

Back at the ranch, Millie sat at the table and stared at the permit again. The paper looked official, strong, unbending. She traced the stamped seal with her fingertip.

We just got the land, she thought, and now we're bringing a child onto it.

Clem set a mug of coffee beside her. Not because it was cold, but because it was something steady to hold. He didn't say much. He just stayed there, close enough to mean it.

* * *

THE BIRTH DIDN'T COME with soft music or clean sheets. It came with cabin heat and hard timing, the kind that stacked up from a July sun that wouldn't let go, and a stove you still had to run. The iron box stayed lit for boiling water, not comfort, and the kettle never cooled. Every towel Millie owned was washed twice and still looked worn. The air in the cabin turned thick, heavy with heat, and the sharp mix of soap, sweat, and woodsmoke that clung to everything. Clem moved through the room like a man trying to outwork fear. He scrubbed his hands until his knuckles went raw, then scrubbed them again.

The midwife arrived from a neighboring spread just before dusk, face flushed from the ride and the long day, dust clinging to her skirts and the creases of her hands. Older. Calm. She didn't waste words, she'd seen too much to be impressed. She set her bag on the table, then took one look at Millie and nodded.

"All right," she said. "Let's do this." And she showed Millie how to breathe through the pains.

Millie gripped the edge of the mattress and breathed like she'd been taught, until breathing wasn't enough. The pain came in waves that stole her voice and wouldn't give it back. Clem stayed close, offering water, cloth, his hand, his prayers. Millie could see it on him, the helplessness, in the way he kept stepping in and stopping again. She saw it in his jaw, too, in the way he started forward, then stopped, like he didn't know where to put himself.

"It's all right," she whispered once, between contractions, and the words were for him as much as for herself. "Just stay."

He did. He stayed until his legs shook and his heart felt too big for his chest.

The midwife worked with steady hands and a voice that didn't rise. "Now," she said, when the moment came. "Right now, Millie. Give me everything you've got."

Millie did. She bore down and the world narrowed to heat, effort, and the sound of her own breath. Clem hovered like he was standing on the edge of something, close enough to see the storm, too far to stop it.

Then, sudden and sharp, the baby arrived.

Healthy. Loud. Angry at the cold air. Perfect.

That first cry changed Clem. His shoulders dropped like he'd been holding up the roof. His eyes went wet, and he didn't even try to hide it. He stared at the small squirming life in the midwife's hands like he didn't trust it to be real.

Millie's relief hit hard and fierce. She sobbed once, then laughed through it, like her body couldn't choose a single emotion big enough. She reached for the baby with trembling hands, pulling him close, feeling warmth, weight, and heartbeat.

"A boy," the midwife said, satisfied.

Millie looked up at Clem, hair damp at her temples, face exhausted and shining all at once. "What are we going to name him?"

Clem swallowed. He looked at the baby, then at Millie, then down at the floor like the answer might be hiding there. When he spoke, his voice was soft.

"A Bible name," he said. "Something solid. Like John."

Millie smiled, slow and full. "John," she repeated, tasting it. Then she looked at Clem like she'd just been handed hope. "Baby John."

And just like that, it was true. They had a baby. They had a boy. And hard country or not, the cabin suddenly felt like the safest place in the world.

People always say time flies when you're having fun. Millie used to think that was something folks said at picnics, with lemonade and clean hands. Out here, it turned out to be true anyway. Not because life was easy, but because it never stopped moving.

A whole year passed, stitched together from chores, weather, and small victories that didn't look like much until you added them up.

They found a routine, the kind you fall into when there's no other choice. Millie worked with Baby John close by, in a basket or on a quilt, or toddling underfoot like a little shadow. She was always watching, always tired, and somehow still standing. She'd learned to stir beans with one hand and keep the other ready, just in case.

Clem built and fixed and hauled, the ranch turning into a long list that never got shorter. He patched fences, split wood, and carried feed as if grit alone could keep them afloat. But the boy changed him. Not all at once, and not politely. Clem was teaching himself to soften, one laugh at a time. Some days he'd catch the sound of Baby John giggling and freeze, listening to the sweetest sounds he had ever heard.

John was just over one now, curious and bold, a kid who wanted to be where danger lived. If a gate was open, he headed for it. If a bucket was full, he wanted to look. If the dog barked, he crawled toward the noise with that fearless grin.

The chores didn't care that they were a family now. Water still had to be hauled. Fences still had to be checked. Feed still had to be measured. Repairs still had to be done before the next storm could finish what the last one started. Money stayed tight, always in the background like a low ache.

They'd gathered a small collection of animals along the way. A handful of chickens that Millie fussed over like they were her children. A few hogs that ate like every meal was their last. And one nervous horse Clem had gotten in a trade, work for a neighbor, a bargain that looked better on paper than it did in the corral.

Still, the place had started to feel like a home. Settled. Normal, if you didn't look too closely.

The morning began like every other morning before it. Quiet. Familiar.

And ordinary, right up until it wasn't.

Clem decided that today was the day.

That saddle was going on that horse, no matter what.

He'd been circling the problem for weeks, tightening the cinch, loosening it, talking low, trying patience as a tool. The horse was still nervous, still jumpy, still acting as if every shadow was a predator. Clem had traded good labor for the animal, and the trade had been fair, but fair didn't mean easy.

Millie stayed inside, cleaning and cooking and running through her list of daily chores. She moved through her morning in small, practiced motions, wiping the table, tending the stove, folding laundry. She even caught herself humming John's favorite songs. This new normal was becoming a life she loved.

John had been walking more and more. He'd taken his first steps at eleven months, and Clem had laughed like a boy himself. Millie had cried and tried to pretend it was just dust in her eyes. Now John treated walking like a new job he planned to master, wobbling one moment, steady the next, always pushing toward whatever looked interesting, dangerous, or off-limits.

That morning was unusually warm. Millie left the front door open to let the fresh air in, and because she liked hearing Clem's boots move across the yard. It made her feel less alone.

John was in a full diaper and no shirt, his belly round, his curly blond hair sticking up in soft tufts. He toddled to the open doorway like it had been left open just for him. He paused at the threshold, blinking at the light, then stepped outside, passing the tin truck on the porch that he loved to push through the dust. He moved with the confidence of someone who didn't know fear yet.

"Da Da," he said.

Clem was in the yard, near the corral, working with the horse. He had his back half-turned, one hand on the saddle, the other steadying the animal's shoulder. He was focused the way he always was when something mattered. Focused enough to miss everything else.

John took a few more steps, drawn to the motion and the sound of Clem's voice. He was quiet, the way small children can be when they're doing something they know they're not supposed to do. He wandered behind the horse, too close, and unseen for one breath too many.

"Da Da," he said again.

It landed in the air at the exact wrong moment.

Clem lifted the saddle and settled it onto the horse's back, firm and sure. The horse flinched, then bucked, fast and violent. A reflex, not evil. Pure instinct, a body rejecting pressure and surprise. Hooves struck dirt, muscle surged, and the animal's hindquarters snapped sideways.

Impact happened in a blink.

Clean. Hard. Final.

Millie didn't understand it at first. Clem moved, fast and wrong, like his body had decided before his mind caught up. She heard the thud, felt the world tilt, then saw the diaper in the dirt, the small shape, the stillness that didn't belong in a yard where life was always moving.

He moved so fast it didn't look like thinking. A sound tore out of him, half shout, half prayer. He dropped the reins, lunged forward, and went to his knees so fast the gravel cut through his pants. His hands were everywhere at once, reaching, turning, checking, as if the right touch could rewind time.

"John," he said, and his voice didn't sound like his own. "Johnny. Hey, hey, hey."

Millie heard the sound. Not the words, not at first, just the raw shape of Clem's voice. Her heart went cold before her feet even moved. She stepped onto the porch, dish towel still in her hand, and saw Clem on the ground.

For one impossible second her mind refused it. It offered other explanations. A fall. A bump. A scare that would end with crying.

Then she saw John.

The yard went unnaturally quiet. Even the horse stopped, sides heaving, ears flicking like it didn't know what it had done. The wind seemed to hold its breath. The morning light kept shining, like it had no idea it should dim.

There was no crying. No movement. Just silence, breath, and dirt.

Millie's legs tried to fold. She made a sound that wasn't a word and stumbled off the porch, one hand reaching out as if she could pull the scene back into the cabin, back into safety, back into yesterday.

Clem looked up at her, eyes wide and ruined, and she knew, before he said anything, that their ordinary morning was gone.

Clem rushed into motion like motion could fix it.

He scooped John up, shouting for Millie, telling her to get the blanket, get the keys, get in the truck. His hands shook so hard he could barely hold the child, but he held him anyway, tight like refusal. The engine roared to life and the tires threw dirt as if speed could buy mercy.

Millie sat beside him, one hand braced on the dash, the other on John's blanket, as if touching cloth could warm what had gone cold. The road into town was rutted and long. Clem drove like he was chasing a miracle, eyes locked ahead, jaw locked harder. Every bump felt like an apology he couldn't say fast enough.

At the small county hospital, the doctor took one look and his face changed. He moved with care, but not with hope. He checked, listened, pressed, then stood back and met Clem's eyes.

"He died instantly," the doctor said. Plain. Final. "You couldn't have done a thing."

The words hit Millie first. Her body went cold, then hot, then numb, then nothing at all. She didn't cry at first. She couldn't. Her mind floated above her, watching someone else's life come apart.

Clem didn't take the words in like comfort. He took them in like punishment. His head dipped, shoulders tight, and you could see the spiral start behind his eyes. "I should've... I should've... I should've..." An endless sentence, with no period and no mercy.

Paperwork followed because paperwork always does. A death certificate. A signature. A stamp. Ink on a page that didn't have the right to exist. The doctor spoke gently, but it didn't matter. Nothing mattered except the fact that John wasn't coming home.

By the next day, The Gazette ran a short report, the kind that filled the bottom corner of a page. A few lines. A name. An age. Words too small for the size of the loss.

Neighbors came by with hushed faces and casseroles that no one could taste. They stood in the yard, hats in hands, offering condolences, offering prayers, offering anything they could carry without breaking. Millie nodded at people and couldn't remember what they said five seconds later.

Not everyone came with kindness.

A relative of Mr. Halverson, still bitter about the land, stood off to the side with another man and talked low, as if tragedy was a lesson and they were the teachers. He quoted Proverbs 20:21 to the man beside him. He got the words wrong, but not the judgment.

"Greed in the beginning," he muttered, "means no blessing."

Clem heard it. Of course he did. He didn't turn. He didn't argue. His jaw clenched so tight a muscle jumped in his cheek. He held himself rigid until he got inside, away from eyes and voices.

Then he folded. Tears from a man that didn't cry. Millie could see he regretted every step that had brought him to this awful day.

Millie watched him from the doorway, still holding John's

blanket, and didn't know which pain was worse, losing her boy, or seeing the man beside her finally admit he couldn't fix everything.

They buried John on their own land because it was the only place that made sense. The county had rules, but grief had stronger ones. Clem chose a spot near the ridge, where the ground rose and the wind never seemed to rest. He chose it with a stiff face and trembling hands, like he was afraid to pick wrong and lose the boy again.

The funeral was small, modest, still. No preacher in a fancy coat. No long speeches. Just a handful of people who showed up because decent folks do. Doris came, her eyes red, holding Millie's hand like she could anchor her. The sheriff stood off to the side, hat in his hands, looking awkward and human. One ranch family came too, kind strangers with a pan of food they'd set down without a word, as if even their kindness didn't want attention.

Millie barely heard what anyone said. The words floated past her like smoke. She kept seeing the open door. She kept seeing John's bare feet on the porch boards. She kept hearing that small voice, "Da Da," like it had been said into a room that would never answer back.

It was her fault, she told herself. She'd looked away. She'd left the door open. She'd assumed the morning was safe because it looked like every other morning.

Clem didn't say much either. He stood beside her like a post in the ground, but his eyes looked hollow. Millie could see the blame on him anyway, in the way he wouldn't meet her gaze, in the way his jaw stayed tight like he was holding something back. It sat on his shoulders like weight, the horse, the trade, the permit, the ranch, the whole plan. He held himself like he'd wanted this land so badly he'd dragged them into it, and now it had taken something back.

They didn't have the strength to fight about it. There was no heat left for blame that could land on the other person. They each absorbed the guilt, carrying the weight alone.

When it was time, Clem lowered the small bundle into the earth, hands shaking so badly Doris stepped closer, just in case. Clem's face tightened, and then the tears came, sudden and brutal. Not pretty crying. Not a single tear wiped away with pride. Wrecked crying, the kind that shakes a man down to the bone, the kind that makes the air hurt going in and out. He pressed his fist to his mouth like he could hold the sound in, but it broke out anyway. Millie had seen him upset, seen him angry, seen him scared in tight, controlled ways. She'd never seen him cry like this. Not even right after it happened. This was worse. It wasn't the clean kind of crying. It was breaking.

Millie turned her face away, not out of pride, but out of fear. If Clem could fall apart, then the whole world might be as fragile as it felt.

When it was done, they lingered a moment longer. The ridge looked out over miles of land that didn't care. The wind still moved. A crow called from somewhere far off. The sky stayed wide.

Then they walked back down toward the cabin.

The world hadn't stopped. The chores still waited. And the emptiness followed them home.

Days blurred into each other, soft at the edges and cruel in the middle. Morning came. Night came. The space in between felt like a long hallway with no doors.

Clem cried every day. Quietly. Not the wrecked kind from the burial, but the steady kind, like grief had become a habit. He'd sit on the edge of the bed with his back to Millie, shoulders moving, trying not to disturb the dead, or the living.

He built a small family cemetery around where John was buried. Split rails, posts set deep, corners squared, as if straight lines could bring order to what had happened. The spot was near the ridge, looking out over the valley.

On the day he nailed down the last rail, his hammer slowed, then stopped. He stared at the wood like he'd forgotten what it was for. His face went hard, silent, lost somewhere Millie couldn't reach. He stayed that way a long time, standing still with the hammer hanging from his hand.

After John went into the ground, Clem did ranch work because he didn't know how to stop. He kept working because stopping felt impossible. But he wasn't really there. He moved like a man following instructions in a language he didn't understand.

So Millie became the backbone, because there was no other option.

She handled the animals, the food, even some of the repairs. She kept track of bills and the land permit requirements, making sure the place stayed presentable for whatever inspection might come next. She kept the ranch alive while her heart felt buried right beside that little grave.

Millie wanted to fall apart. Some mornings she woke up and thought, I can't do this. Then she did it anyway.

One afternoon she grabbed a shovel and walked out past the cabin, past the corral, past where the grass thinned. She picked a spot and started digging. Two hours of dirt, sweat, and muscle. She didn't stop to rest. She didn't stop to think.

When the hole was deep enough, she stood there, breathing hard, staring into it like it might answer her. The soft blanket she'd held her child in from birth slipped into the hole wet with tears.

Then she covered it back in, one shovel of earth at a time. John was buried near the ridge but Millie put some of his memories from inside her where it could not be retrieved.

* * *

Millie stood alone at the small grave, wind pressing into her face like it had something to say. Her hands were raw from work and weather, her nails rimmed with dirt she couldn't scrub away. The split-rail fence creaked behind her, and the valley stretched out wide and indifferent.

She didn't pray in fancy words. She didn't try to make it pretty.

She spoke one honest truth out loud, the kind that didn't need poetry to hurt.

"This is our land," she said. Her voice shook, but it held. "We will pass it on to our family. Our family."

The wind took the words and carried them off like a promise that didn't belong to her alone anymore.

She walked back down to the cabin and found Clem inside, sitting with his elbows on his knees, staring at nothing. He looked up like he'd forgotten how to expect anyone to come back.

Millie crossed the room and cupped his face in both hands. She held him still and made him meet her eyes.

They cried, both of them, quiet at first, then not so quiet. Millie's tears weren't only grief. They were anger too, and fear, and the stubborn refusal to lose everything.

"This is how it is now," she whispered. "This ranch isn't a plan. It's a way of life. Quitting would be another death."

Clem didn't magically heal. His eyes stayed wrecked. His mouth trembled. But he heard her. He nodded slowly, small and real. His hand closed around hers, the only solid thing left.

"Okay," he said, and it sounded like surrender and agreement all at the same time.

That evening on the porch, they noticed the tin truck again, the one they'd paid too much for at a yard sale in town. It sat near the door, catching the last of the light.

As the sun went down, looking out over the land, they held hands and realized that the chores didn't care what they'd lost.

Tomorrow was another day.

CHAPTER EIGHT

THE EMPTY ROOM

Several months passed after John died. The days didn't get kinder, they just got organized again.

The ranch fell back into its old rhythm. Not happy. Not whole. Just workable. Feed at dawn. Water checked. A saddle thrown over a rail. Dishes done before the sun set. Routine that kept you moving even when you didn't want to.

Clem started coming back to his old self in pieces.

At first it was small. He ate more than a few bites. He shaved without Millie reminding him. One morning he spoke first, a simple "Coffee's on," as if it wasn't a big deal, as if it didn't take effort to push the words out.

Then he began taking on more. He walked the fence line without being asked. He tightened wire. He replaced a post that had been leaning since spring. He brought in firewood before the weather turned, stacking it neat, like he'd always done it.

Millie should've felt relief.

Instead, the house felt emptier.

When Clem had been broken open and quiet, she'd moved through the rooms like they were the only thing keeping him together. Now, with him stepping back into the work, there were minutes at a time where she didn't know what to do with her hands. Silence stretched. The air felt colder, even on warm afternoons.

For days now, she'd closed her eyes as she stepped onto the porch.

The tin truck still sat outside near the door. When they bought it, they'd laughed about the cost like they had money to waste. If she looked at it too long, her chest tightened and she felt like she might sit down and never get back up. So she didn't look. She counted steps instead.

Inside, John's baby room stayed exactly the same. The little blanket still folded on the chair. The empty crib. The clean-linen smell that no longer made sense.

Millie paused in the doorway one morning and realized something that scared her.

She could almost breathe again.

And she hated herself for it.

However, today was different.

Millie didn't plan it. There wasn't a decision made over breakfast, no moment where she told herself, *This is the day.* She just found herself on the porch with the tin truck in her hands.

It felt heavier than it should've. She carried it inside and found herself drawn back to John's room.

She stood there a long second, staring at the baby room door like it might talk back to her. The house was quiet, not peaceful, just empty.

Millie opened the door and stepped inside alone.

She walked to the crib and set the tin truck on the edge, right there on the rail like it belonged. Like John might reach for it.

Millie sat down. The chair creaked under her, and she hated the sound because it proved she was still here.

She picked the truck back up. Held it to her chest.

Her face didn't twist. She didn't wail. She just folded in on herself, quiet but complete. Tears came before she could stop them. Her shoulders shook. Her mouth opened without a sound. Grief filled the room, and for the first time she let it.

The ranch had kept her busy enough to survive. All the chores. Tasks stacked on tasks until there wasn't room left to think.

Now there was room.

Outside, she heard Clem. A hammer hit wood. A gate clanked. His boots crossed the yard. He was working. He was recovering. The sound of him moving forward hit her wrong, like she was all alone now.

Millie stood up too fast and the chair scraped the floor.

She shut the door.

Then she stopped with her hand on the knob.

She opened it again.

Like closing it made it worse. Like leaving it open made it worse too.

Millie went back to the crib, grabbed the tin truck, and walked out with it clutched tight.

She crossed to the kitchen, lifted the trash lid, and threw it in.

The truck landed with a dull clank.

Millie stared at the bin like she expected to feel better.

She didn't.

She just put the lid down slow and stood there, breathing through it, like breathing was the only job she could manage. The truck lay in the dark at the bottom of the bin. She couldn't bring herself to touch it.

Clem started insisting on more chores.

"I got it," he'd say, already pulling on his coat. "You sit a minute."

He fixed a sagging hinge. Hauled water. Checked the far fence. He acted like work could balance a scale that didn't exist.

Millie let him.

Partly because she was tired all the way through. Partly because she was proud of him, proud he was moving again, proud he was trying. She didn't say that out loud. She just nodded and watched him go.

With less on her hands, her mind got louder.

A day stretched too long. The clock ticked. It seemed louder than normal. She craved the silence, and she hated it at the same time.

Millie found herself staring at the road more than once, waiting on something that wasn't coming. A little laugh. A small cry. The quick slap of bare feet on a porch board. She'd blink and realize she'd been holding her breath.

She went back into the baby room and started grabbing things.

A tiny shirt. A soft blanket. The little cap she'd washed twice before he ever wore it. She carried them to the kitchen and dropped them in the trash. Just like she did with the tin truck.

Then she stood there, hands shaking, and pulled them right back out.

She smoothed the blanket like it wasn't garbage. The way you handled something that still mattered. Like she could undo what had happened if she folded it right.

Millie shoved the items back in the room, then paused in the doorway, ashamed and angry at the same time.

She didn't know what she was supposed to do with love that had nowhere to land.

Then Clem shifted.

Not in a loud way. Not enough that anyone in town would've noticed. But Millie noticed, because she lived close to him, because she'd watched every change since John.

He started leaving earlier.

Before the light was fully up, she'd hear boots, a low clink of tack, then the porch boards and the gate. Some days he wasn't back until late, when the sky had already started fading.

When he came inside, his answers were short.

"Fence line."

"Over by the sale barn."

"Had to handle something."

His pockets were tight, like they held more than a pocketknife and twine. Not bulging, just heavy. He'd empty them in the bedroom with his back turned, then wash up like he was trying to scrub something off that wasn't dirt.

She noticed little things.

A different saddle tied off, one she didn't remember him using since the old days. A faint smell on his shirt that wasn't their barn. The sound of a truck on the road that didn't match the usual traffic, then the quick hush after it passed.

One afternoon she saw Clem at the pump, hands under the water longer than normal. He rubbed at his palms and nails like something might still be there.

Millie asked simple questions while she worked.

"Who was that on the road?"

"Just a fella passing through," Clem said.

"What'd you do all the way out past the north fence?"

"Checked for washouts. Took longer than I thought."

"Why'd you need the good saddle?"

He didn't look at her right away. "Just wanted to ride something that wouldn't throw me."

The answers were careful. Too careful. Like he'd practiced them on the walk back.

Millie watched him while he ate, while he stared at his plate, while he kept his voice steady. Behind his eyes she saw something old, something he'd promised was gone. The part of him that could talk smooth, move fast, and make a deal sound harmless.

That night, near dusk, she thought she heard something.

Not the usual sounds from the far pasture. This was different. It started as a low restless noise. Then it got louder, and louder.

Millie went to the window and listened.

Clem stayed at the table, chewing slow, like he hadn't heard a thing. He wasn't surprised, and that scared her more than the noise.

Then she heard them before she saw them. All of them. Hooves across the field. Three large trucks were already pulling away, and a few cowboys were still pushing cattle through the gate.

She stepped off the porch and walked toward the pasture, keeping to the fence line. The ground was churned up near the gate, hoofprints everywhere. Fresh droppings. A few tufts of hair caught on the wire.

When she topped the small rise, she stopped cold.

Cattle. A lot of them.

They were spread across the grass, still settling, heads up, nervous energy moving through the herd. Millie started counting without meaning to, the way you do when your brain is trying to prove you're wrong.

Ten. Twenty. Thirty.

She kept going, walking the fence, counting again because the first count couldn't be right.

By the time she finished, her stomach had dropped into a hard knot.

One hundred head, give or take.

They didn't own cattle. They were just broke. Flat broke.

She stood there gripping the top wire, eyes scanning brands she didn't recognize, trying to find any sign this made sense.

She heard the screen door creak behind her, then the porch boards.

Behind her, boots on dry ground.

Clem came up like he'd been out there the whole time, calm as Sunday.

"You see?" he said. "Ain't that something?"

Millie turned fast. "What is this?"

Clem kept his hands easy at his sides. "It's good news."

"Don't you say that like it's normal," she snapped, and she

pointed toward the pasture. "Clem, there's a hundred head of cattle on our land."

He nodded once, like that matched his plan. "Right."

"Whose are they?"

Clem looked past her for a second, then back. "It's a handshake deal."

Millie stared at him. "A handshake deal for a hundred head?"

"It's temporary."

"Temporary doesn't answer my question," she said. Her voice stayed level, but she could feel heat climbing up her neck. "Let's do the math, Clem. You want to pretend we're ranchers now, fine. I can do numbers."

He didn't interrupt, which told her plenty.

"Two hundred and fifty dollars a head," she said, loud enough the cattle could hear her. "That's being generous. A hundred head. That's twenty-five thousand dollars worth of cattle."

Clem shifted his weight. "They ain't paid for like that."

"We don't have anything close to that," Millie went on. "We don't have twenty-five thousand. We don't have five thousand. We've got bills, we've got feed, we've got repairs. We've got grief, if you want to be honest."

Millie stepped closer. "So I'll ask it plain. Whose cattle are these, Clem?"

He opened his mouth, then closed it. He looked toward the pasture again, like the answer might be written on a hide.

Millie's anger arrived clean and sharp.

"I'm not living on stolen goods," she said through clenched teeth. "Not after everything. Not after John. Not after what we promised each other."

Clem held up a hand, not to stop her, but like he was trying to slow the whole situation down. "They ain't stolen."

"Then talk," Millie said. "Right now."

Clem exhaled and finally gave her the pitch, the one he'd been holding back, offered up like a gift.

"We don't have to buy cattle outright," he said. "Not yet. Plenty of folks got cows and no grass, or they're stretched thin and can't carry 'em through the season. We've got plenty of grass for grazing. And that permit paperwork I've been pushing since the commissioner came through, it finally went our way. So we do it on shares."

Millie didn't blink.

"We take their cows in," Clem continued, voice steady, practiced. "We run 'em, we salt 'em, we watch 'em, we doctor what needs doctoring. They don't hand us cash. They hand us cattle. Come fall, we get calves. It's sweat, Millie. It's grass turned into money."

Millie listened, and the more he talked, the more familiar it sounded. Not the cattle part. The way he said it. The way it slid across rough edges.

She shook her head. "You don't get to make a deal like that without me."

"I'm trying to fix a problem," he said quickly.

"That's what you said back then," Millie snapped. "That same tone. That same careful talking."

Clem's eyes hardened a little. "This is different."

"Then tell me the names," Millie said. "The terms. When do they leave, what do we owe, what do we get, and what happens if something goes wrong? Who's responsible if one dies, or if one wanders onto someone else's place?"

Clem hesitated, just long enough.

Millie took a step closer, keeping her voice low now. "Whose cattle, Clem?"

He swallowed. "It's a guy I know from the auction barn. I'm helping him out."

Millie stared at him, waiting for the rest.

"What's his name?" she asked again.

Clem didn't answer right away, and the cattle kept bawling behind them like they were part of the argument. He turned away without answering.

The cattle didn't care what Millie wanted.

They needed water. They needed the fence checked and tightened where they'd already leaned on it. Salt blocks set out. Heads counted again because one hundred looked different every time they shifted.

Millie followed, but she stayed mad, and it helped.

Anger burned clean and hot, and it kept her moving. She hauled buckets like she was trying to wear the day out. She walked the fence line fast, eyes sharp, hands steady on wire and staples. She dropped salt where it needed to go and didn't stop to think about anything else.

Clem tried to take over.

"Millie, I'll handle it," he said, reaching for the bucket.

She jerked it back. "No."

He stared at her, surprised.

She didn't soften. "You brought 'em here, you don't get to do this without me too."

So they worked side by side.

Short sentences. Quick hand signals. A point toward a corner post. Two fingers up for a count. A nod when something was done. No romance in it, no extra words, just partnership that meant survival.

Clem stayed quiet. Millie stayed focused.

By late afternoon, her shoulders ached and her hands were raw. The herd had water. The fence held. The gate latched clean.

Millie stood at the edge of the yard and realized something that made her pause.

She'd made it through the whole afternoon without walking into the empty room.

After dark, the house felt smaller.

Clem sat at the table with a plate he didn't touch, elbows on the wood like it could hold him up. Millie moved around the kitchen slow, not from tiredness, from control. She wanted her words steady.

When she finally sat down across from him, she didn't ease into it.

"The cattle don't get to be a secret," she said. "Not in this marriage."

Clem's eyes lifted to hers. He didn't argue. That alone told her he knew how far he'd stepped.

"I wasn't trying to hurt you," he said.

"That's not the point," Millie replied. "You don't get to make deals that can take this place from us, then act like it's fine."

He swallowed, then nodded. "I'm trying to build something solid again, Millie. Fast. Before the permit deadlines. Before something else hits us."

Millie leaned forward, voice low. "Don't turn this into a speech. I don't need noble. I need straight."

Clem's jaw tightened. He looked down at his hands, then back up. "Alright."

"Clean rules," Millie said. "No more cash deals without me knowing. No more surprises. Not one. If a decision can cost us the land, it's both of us, every time."

Clem nodded once, then again, slower. "You're right."

Millie watched him, making sure the words landed.

Clem stared at the table a second longer than he needed to. His eyes went distant for a beat, and Millie didn't like it. He looked like a man thinking about someone else, someone who could make trouble. She'd seen that look before, the one that meant there was more to the story than he was giving.

Clem finally met her eyes. "From here on out, you know everything."

Millie waited until Clem went to bed.

Then she walked down the hall and stopped at the baby room door. Her hand rested on the knob, and she didn't hesitate this time.

Inside, the room was the same, but she wasn't.

She didn't sit. She didn't fold into herself. She stepped in, breathed once, then crossed to the chair and straightened one thing, just one. The folded blanket, corners nudged back into place. Not a fix. Not a statement. Just a small act she could control.

Millie stood there a moment longer, letting the air settle in her chest.

Outside, cattle shifted in the dark. A low murmur. Hooves on ground. The steady sounds of living responsibility that didn't stop just because her heart wanted it to.

It didn't erase anything.

But it kept her in the present.

Millie turned off the light and closed the door, gentle this time. She didn't lock it away. She just left it.

Back in the kitchen, she looked out into the night, listening to the herd, thinking about permits and fences, and men who showed up with handshake deals.

Tomorrow wasn't just another day anymore.

Tomorrow had teeth.

CHAPTER NINE

THE SURE THING

Time passed in hard, ordinary days. Two years had gone by since their son John died, and the ranch kept moving because it had to. Seasons changed, work stacked up, and nobody asked permission for grief.

The Spyker place began to look like a real operation. More fence line held. The routine tightened. There were fewer nights where Millie lay awake counting bills and listening for bad news at the door. She grew tougher, not because she wanted to, but because the work demanded it. The loss stayed with her, even on the good days.

* * *

CLEM SETTLED back into what he understood best. He still worked like any ranch hand, but he also watched the numbers, watched the neighbors, and planned ahead. He started playing the long game again.

His cattle deal did what he promised it would do. The herd became theirs, piece by piece. The money wasn't rich, but it was steady enough to buy feed on time, fix what broke, and breathe without feeling guilty about it.

Millie insisted on knowing everything. So, Clem showed her the books at the kitchen table, then pushed them aside and used what he trusted more, simple ranch math.

"Prices move," he said. "Not because it's fair, but because it's what folks do."

He explained it as plainly as he could. "When everyone hauls cattle to town at the same time, the pens get full. Buyers take their time, lean back, act picky. The price drops because nobody's in a hurry except the seller."

Millie nodded, so Clem continued, "When cattle are scarce, it flips. Buyers get jumpy. They start bidding earlier, bidding higher, because they don't know what's coming next week."

It was like a light clicked on in her head. She was starting to get it. "A rancher can't set the price," Clem said. "All he can do is choose when he walks in that ring."

Millie listened, nodding at the right spots. She was impressed by how quick he was with it, and uneasy at how calm he sounded. It felt less like talk and more like a plan forming right in front of her.

Clem tapped the table once. "We don't have to be the smartest," he said. "We just can't be the most desperate."

Clem hadn't been back to that auction barn in years. Not since a deal that should've stayed buried. He told himself it was smarter to keep his head down now, keep the ranch clean, keep Millie out of anything that could stain her name.

Then he showed up anyway.

The barn hit him the same as always, dust in the air, old boards underfoot, burnt coffee, and men talking without really talking. The ring kept moving, the chant rolling, and the money changing hands as if it were nothing.

He spotted the helper near the gate, the one everybody knew. The kind who carried a clipboard but somehow always knew

DUST AND INHERITANCE

more than the clipboard did. Easy smile. Patient eyes. He watched the pens, watched the buyers, watched Clem.

The helper's gaze landed and stayed. He sized Clem up fast, a man who'd built something up, still hungry, still proud enough to think he could handle the heat.

The helper drifted close, casual as smoke. "You didn't hear this from me," he said.

Clem knew what that meant. Information had a price, and it never came without strings.

He shouldn't have reached for his pocket. He did anyway.

The cash changed hands quick and quiet, like it had been practiced. The helper's smile didn't change, but his eyes did. Clem walked out with "knowledge" in his pocket, and a familiar feeling in his chest.

Old Clem was awake again.

But he didn't jump all in. He made it a test, a small group of cattle, nothing that would break them if it went sideways. He took the knowledge he got from the helper. Then he picked the day the way a man picked a lock, careful and quiet.

The barn was lighter than usual, fewer pens filled, more buyers standing close to the rail. Clem watched their boots, their hands, how quick they leaned forward when a good steer came through. Hungry buyers were different. They didn't waste time.

When Clem's cattle hit the ring, the bids climbed faster than he expected. Not by a fortune, but enough to matter. Enough to turn a tight month into a steady one. He kept his face flat, nodded once, signed what needed signing, and walked out as if it were just another sale.

Inside, something sparked. The old part of him. The part that loved timing and leverage, loved being the one who knew.

He found the helper again before he left town. The cash went across easy, like payment and promise all at once. Clem told himself it was practical. He wanted the next edge.

* * *

BACK AT THE RANCH, Millie saw how much better that last sale was. She let herself enjoy it, just a little, because relief felt rare. Then she watched Clem carefully that night. He'd started looking past her, as if he was measuring something.

"One good sale can change a whole year," Clem said that night.

Millie nodded, but a quiet thought followed behind it.

Or ruin it.

The second tip didn't call for a cautious test. It called for a real move.

Clem loaded more cattle. He didn't say much about it, just that he'd been watching the market. Millie noticed the way he said it, confident, certain, as if the outcome was already decided.

At the barn, the timing hit again. Buyers showed up ready, numbers tight, bids stronger. The sale cleared better than the first, not by pennies, but by enough to change what the ranch could do next. Clem didn't relax once, not when the bids climbed, not when the numbers landed.

Nobody celebrated that night. The barn cut the checks, the bank held the funds, and Clem made Millie sit with him at the table and run the numbers over and over. He wrote out what had to get paid first. Taxes. Feed. Notes.

By the time the money actually cleared, they already had a plan.

The money started solving problems that had been waiting in line for years. Old bills got paid without stretching due dates. Feed and salt got bought before they ran low. Repairs that Clem used to patch with wire and stubbornness got hired out. A tractor showed up in the yard, used but solid, and it made the work faster in a way Millie could feel by the end of the day.

She was grateful. She was also not blind.

That night, she asked him straight. "How do you know it's not just timing and coincidence?"

Clem didn't flinch. "Because I'm not guessing," he said. "I'm choosing the moment. I'm watching what other men do, and I'm not doing it with them."

He made it sound like skill, like discipline, like he'd finally found the honest way to get ahead. Millie wanted to believe him, but she'd learned that certainty could be its own problem.

Then the helper started showing up more, not on the ranch, but in Clem's talk. Clem mentioned him by name, mentioned what he'd "heard," mentioned the next sale before the last one felt fully real.

The helper also changed. He stopped acting like a man doing a favor. He acted familiar now, smiling as if they shared something. He called Clem "partner" once, a joke on the surface, then watched to see if Clem corrected him.

Clem didn't.

After the third conversation, Clem stood at the sink, staring out the window at the yard lights and the tractor parked under them. "Just one more time," he said, more to himself than to her. "Bigger. Then we're truly safe."

Millie didn't answer right away.

She was trying to figure out when "safe" had started to sound like a reason to gamble.

A week later, Clem brought it up casual as breath, the way you called out tomorrow's chores.

"I've got one more sale," he said. "It's a sure thing."

Millie didn't look up from the counter at first. She kept her hands busy, because she didn't trust what her face would do. Then she turned.

"No," she said. One word, flat and final.

Clem blinked, like he hadn't expected the hit. "Millie, I'm not guessing. I'm watching the market. I'm picking the right day. That's all this is."

"That's what you said before," she shot back. "Different words, same promise."

He tried to keep it calm. He used ranch talk, the kind that sounded clean. Timing. Cycles. Demand. He talked about buyers and supply as if it were weather, and he was just smart enough to read the sky.

Millie stepped closer. "You don't get to dress it up and call it honest," she said. "I know what it sounds like when you're sure."

Clem shook his head. "This isn't some con."

"Then why does it feel like one?" Her voice rose. "Because it ends the same way. You go bigger. You get bolder. Then you tell me not to worry."

He opened his mouth, then paused, and that pause told her more than his words did.

"I sold the house in town," he said.

Millie froze. Clem's little house in town, the one he'd owned before she came along, was gone. It had been their quiet fallback, the place they could go if the ranch ever broke them.

"You did what?" she said, and the fear hit behind the anger.

"We weren't using it," Clem said, too quick. "It was sitting there costing us money. I turned it into cash."

"That was our safety," she said. "You don't throw that away."

"It's not throwing it away," he snapped. "It's moving it where it works."

Millie's hands shook. "That's what desperate men do, Clem. They pull up the ladder and swear they're fine."

He reached for the same line again. "Only one more time."

Millie heard it for what it was.

"Tell me what you're risking," she said.

Clem waved it off. "Nothing. No risk at all."

Millie stared at him, furious and sick all at once, because men who said that were always the ones betting the most.

* * *

Clem went to the bank on a Tuesday, another errand on the list. The banker met him with a firm handshake and a calm face, the kind that never showed surprise. Still, his eyes stayed sharp. He listened close when Clem talked about cattle, timing, and "one more strong sale."

The banker didn't argue. He didn't warn him off. He simply laid out terms, neat and clean, and slid the papers across the desk.

Borrowing against the ranch felt different to Clem than borrowing against himself. The land was solid. The herd was real. He told himself he wasn't taking a risk, he was using what he'd built. He signed like a man locking in a win.

* * *

Millie found out that night.

Not from Clem, not straight. She heard it in a comment, then pulled the truth out of him piece by piece. The room went cold. This wasn't raised voices and then sleep, this was something breaking between them.

"This land is our life," she said, steady and shaking at the same time. "And you're putting it on a card table."

Clem tried to answer with numbers. He talked about interest, margins, what the next sale could cover. He promised it was controlled.

Millie didn't fight him after that. She went quiet, and the quiet had weight. She turned away and started clearing the table, slow and exact, as if she had to keep moving to stay upright.

Clem stood there a moment, like his own words had trapped him.

He might've crossed the line.

* * *

Clem met the helper behind the auction barn, away from the ring and the main doors, where men could talk without looking like they were talking. Clem didn't ease into it this time.

"I need a quick turnaround on fifteen thousand," Clem said.

The helper's smile stayed easy. "Costs more when you're in a hurry."

"How much?"

"Twenty-five percent of the take," the helper said, like he was reading a menu. "No arguing."

Clem thought about it for only a moment. He should've walked. Instead, he nodded once.

The helper leaned in just enough to make it feel private. "Big buyer's coming in Saturday," he said. "He'll run the bids up. One day only. You buy Thursday or Friday, then you sell Saturday."

Clem left with his mind already working. Back at the ranch, he treated it like an operation. He checked every head they could move. He sorted by weight and condition. He watched the forecast, counted the miles, and planned the load so the cattle would arrive steady, not stressed. He picked the hour they'd roll out, before daylight, before the roads got busy.

Thursday hit clean and cold. He went in with cash and nerve. The buying moved fast. Pens opened, numbers got called, hands went up. Fifteen thousand disappeared in a hurry, traded for a few head to round out the load.

Saturday was louder. More trucks. More men at the rail. The helper was there, acting like they were strangers. Clem stayed planted near the ring, calm on the outside, tracking bids and faces. When Clem's mixed load came through, the barn shifted. Buyers leaned forward. The bidding climbed quick.

By the time the last head sold, Clem had a total that didn't feel real. Fifty thousand, all told. And he knew exactly what twenty-five percent of it would cost him.

He drove home with the sale receipt in his pocket, proud and relieved, convinced he'd fixed what had been tightening around them for years. He laid it on the table like proof.

Millie stared at it a long moment. Relief hit first, sharp and unwanted, because she could already see what it would pay. Then the anger followed right behind it.

The win didn't erase what he'd risked to get it.

*　*　*

THE HELPER SHOWED up at the house like he belonged there. He leaned against the fence, easy smile, eyes too calm. Something about him pulled Millie straight back to her first days in Montana, men who acted friendly while they measured what they could take.

He asked for Clem by name.

Millie stayed inside, close to the window. She heard something that made her stomach drop.

She thought she heard the helper say, "No delays." That meant they owed him money for something.

Millie started for the door, then stopped. Clem's voice was low, steady, trying to keep it light. He offered time, promised soon, talked like this was still between two reasonable men.

The helper stepped closer, and his tone changed. "You owe me."

Not a request. A demand.

They moved toward the barn, where Millie couldn't hear the words anymore, only the rhythm of them. Clem stood too still. The helper stood too close. Millie watched their shoulders, their hands, the way Clem didn't look at the house.

She understood one thing clearly.

They were in someone else's hands now.

Later that week, Clem spread the cash across the kitchen table, counted and recounted, as if the numbers might change.

Fifty thousand dollars. He stared at the money like it was already gone.

Millie stared at Clem like she was seeing a stranger.

CHAPTER TEN

THE RANCH HOUSE

The next morning, the money was still there.

Bills and bands of cash spread across the kitchen table just like Clem had left it. Millie paused in the doorway with her pan in hand, then set it down and started shifting piles just to make room for breakfast. The paper felt warm from the lamp, and oddly heavy in her fingers, not in weight, but in what it meant. She hated that she had to touch it to crack eggs, hated that it made her careful, like the kitchen suddenly belonged to the bank.

Still, when she stacked the bundles into neat rows, she felt her lungs loosen. Money didn't fix trouble, but it changed the shape of it. It bought feed before the weather turned. It bought nails and boards, not promises. It bought time, which was the one thing they never seemed to have enough of.

Clem tried to act normal. He rinsed his cup, wiped the counter, said nothing about the helper from the auction barn. But his eyes kept cutting toward the window, and every sound outside made his shoulders go tight, like he was waiting on the next knock.

He started shifting the stacks of cash. To Millie it looked like he set aside a quarter of the money.

When Millie didn't speak, he cleared his throat. "I know you heard us. I've got what I owe him."

Millie poured coffee, then set her hands flat on the table.

"We can't live in this shack forever," she said. "Not if we're serious about staying."

His gaze flicked to her, sharp, then softer.

"A real house," she went on. "Not fancy. Just solid. Somewhere we can raise a family. Somewhere that says we're not leaving."

Clem didn't argue. He nodded, fast, like he'd already decided, and was just waiting for her to say it first.

"Yeah," he said. "We'll build. That's something we can do."

Millie watched him stare at the cash. He tightened his jaw, a reflex he always had when he started turning a problem into numbers. He pulled a pencil from the drawer and an old envelope from the junk pile by the sink.

"Fifty," he said under his breath, and wrote it down. "Minus ten for the bank." Another line. "Supplies. Bills." He paused, recalculated, then circled a number.

"Just over thirty," he said, like the sentence tasted both sweet and bitter.

He stared at the table a second longer, like he could see boards and shingles stacked on top of those bills. "Lumber," he muttered. "Delivery. Appliances." His pencil tapped once, then twice. "Stove, fridge. Maybe a washer."

Millie didn't interrupt. Not when he was like this.

"It can be done," he said finally, but his voice dropped at the end. His eyes flicked toward the window, toward the barn, toward the space where the helper seemed to live even when he wasn't there.

"I think it's a really good idea," he said, and the words came quick, like work was safer than the other thing waiting.

Millie didn't talk about the house as a wish. She talked about it as a plan.

"More space," she said, tapping the tabletop with her finger. "A real kitchen, not this corner with a window. Sturdier walls. Better heat. I want us to have a real home."

She said it calmly, but her eyes didn't move when she spoke. She held her ground the same way she did in a hard wind, feet planted, chin level.

After what they'd lost, she couldn't stand the way the place echoed at night. Every creak in the rafters sounded as if it were reminding her of emptiness. She didn't want a house to show off. She wanted a home that didn't feel like a grave you had to live inside.

Clem listened without interrupting. His face stayed neutral, but Millie saw the shift in him, the small respect that flickered when she laid it out in plain terms. He didn't look at her like she was dreaming. He looked at her like she was building something already.

By afternoon she was measuring, scratching notes on paper, sketching a layout with a stub of pencil. She asked questions in town, listened hard, then asked better ones. Neighbors pointed her toward a builder who'd done a place up the road. Millie went to see it and came back describing the stove, the window placement, the way the walls held heat.

Clem did the math again. He kept calculating it over and over. They had enough, on paper.

Millie noticed he got quiet whenever the auction barn was mentioned. He'd pause like he was listening for something in his own head. Still, he indulged himself once, a single purchase that surprised her. A custom belt buckle, polished and fancy, stamped with one word: "SPIKE". It was an old nickname from before Millie, before Montana, before he started pretending his past was gone.

It looked like pride, like a man letting himself believe. Millie didn't know it yet, but that name was going to come back around.

Clem owed the helper a quarter of the take, $12,500. A number that didn't wait politely. Millie didn't know any of the details, but she could feel the tension behind Clem when he spoke to her, the careful way he avoided talking about certain things.

One day while Clem was in town, the helper from the auction barn came by the ranch looking for Clem.

He didn't smile with his eyes. He stood too close to the porch, like he was checking what belonged to him. "Where's Clem?"

Millie kept her voice even, but her skin went cold. "Town" she said.

When Clem got back, she met him at the door.

"That man isn't welcome here again," she said.

Clem didn't ask which man.

He just nodded. "He won't be."

The build started with stakes in frozen ground and the sound of iron biting into dirt.

A crew came out first, boots crunching, breath hanging in the air. Then the deliveries started, lumber stacked in clean piles, a load of nails, sheets of siding, and a stove Millie had picked out like she'd been waiting her whole life to choose one thing that would last. Cold mornings turned into work mornings. The kind where you didn't warm up until you'd already been moving an hour.

Dust rose even in winter. It clung to coats and hair and the inside of Millie's throat. The hammering never really stopped. It started at sunup and chased the daylight until it failed.

Millie came alive in it.

She wasn't standing back watching men do the job. She walked the lines, checked measurements, asked why, then listened. She hauled boards when someone needed a hand. She made decisions fast and didn't apologize for them. Window here, not there. Pantry bigger. Door swung the other way. She learned what a good foundation looked like, and she learned what shortcuts sounded like.

Clem worked like sweat could erase a debt.

He swung a hammer until his hands cracked. He cut, measured, nailed, and lifted like he didn't deserve to sit down. When the builder told him to take a break, he kept going. His eyes were tired, but his body didn't stop, like if he drove enough nails, he could bury the part of himself that still felt owned.

The ranch changed in small, undeniable ways. Not just new boards and fresh framing, but the shape of permanence. A place that looked like it would still be here next winter.

People noticed.

Neighbors rode by slower. Some tipped a hat and said, "Looks good," like they meant it.

Others asked questions that weren't really questions.

"Busy season for you, Clem?"

"Must've been a pretty good sale."

The words were friendly enough, but Millie heard what lived underneath.

Sudden money didn't stay quiet out here. It traveled the same roads as gossip, and it got around before the paint dried.

Clem ran into the helper in town, not by accident, not really.

The helper was standing near the diner, hat tipped back, hands loose at his sides like he had all day. He smiled first. A smile that made a man look harmless, right up until he opened his mouth.

"Morning, Clem."

Clem nodded, kept his face steady. "Morning."

The helper's voice stayed polite, almost friendly, but the words didn't match it. "I need my money."

Clem didn't flinch. "Soon."

"Soon," the helper repeated, like he was tasting it. "That's what you said last time."

Clem tried to keep it light. He pointed toward the street, toward work, toward anything that wasn't this. "Things are moving. I'm getting it lined up."

The helper stepped closer, still smiling. "We had a deal. Deals don't need paper to count."

Clem's chest rose with a tight breath. His hands stayed flat at his sides, fingers stiff like they wanted to curl into fists.

The helper kept talking like they were discussing weather. "Heard you got lumber coming in. Heard there's a foundation started. Folks say you're building yourself a real place out there."

Clem blinked, stayed calm. His eyes didn't even ask why, like he'd been expecting the question.

The helper's smile shifted. Smaller. Meaner. Like a blade turning in the light.

"So you got money to build," he said, soft, "but you don't got money to pay?"

Clem held his gaze. "I'm paying you."

"When?" the helper asked, and the friendliness dropped out of his voice. "Because favors don't stay favors when they're unpaid. They turn into something else."

He leaned in just enough to make it private.

"And you don't want it turning."

By the time Clem left the diner, he could feel eyes on his back. Not just one or two. Half the room saw it when the helper leaned in close, when Clem's smile turned stiff, when the conversation stopped being friendly. People pretended to drink coffee and read menus, but they watched anyway. Out here, you didn't have to hear the words to know trouble.

News didn't travel slow out here. It traveled instantly.

Doris caught Millie later, near the feed store, and didn't waste time.

"Saw Clem in town," she said. "With that man."

Millie felt her stomach drop, then harden. "What man?"

Doris's mouth tightened. "The one that smiles too much."

Millie didn't wait for more.

She found Clem at home and met him in the kitchen, where the new house sketches were pinned to the wall, the white paper bright against the dark wood. She didn't look at them. She looked at him.

"Tell me the truth," she said. "Right now."

Clem tried to soften it. Millie didn't let him.

"How much?" she asked.

He exhaled like it hurt. "Twelve-five."

"And you haven't paid him," she said, not a question.

Clem's eyes dropped. "Not yet."

Fury rushed through her, sharp and clean. "So you made a deal behind my back. You let us start building. You let me plan a future, and you knew we were still tied to him."

"It was for us," Clem said quickly. "For the house. For security."

Millie stepped closer. "You don't buy security by owing the wrong man."

He opened his mouth again, but she cut him off.

"We had a deal," she said. "No more secret deals. No more 'trust me.' Not with land, not with money, not with our lives."

Her voice shook once, then steadied.

"You promised me on our wedding day," she added. "You said we'd do this together."

Clem stood there, the fight draining out of him. His shoulders sagged like the words finally landed where they were supposed to.

"I know," he said, quiet. "You're right."

The house kept going up, but it didn't feel the same.

The framing rose clean and square. The roofline started to show itself against the sky. You could stand in what would be the kitchen and see where the window would go, where the table would sit, where warmth might finally stay put. Millie tried to hold on to that. She stayed busy, stayed sharp, stayed focused on what was right in front of her, because it was the only good thing in motion.

But the joy had thinned.

Clem had changed. He still worked hard, but he worked jumpy. He watched the road while he hammered. He stopped and listened at odd moments, like he was waiting on tires in the distance. In town, his eyes moved too fast, scanning faces, reading the space around him instead of the shelves.

The helper wasn't there, and somehow that made it worse. His presence hung over everything anyway, like a shadow you couldn't step out of.

One afternoon, a man rode up that Clem didn't recognize. Not a neighbor he'd spoken to, not a hand from the sale barn. He sat on his horse easy, like he belonged on the road, and smiled like he was bringing news.

"I was at the auction the other day," he said. "Heard you're building."

Clem nodded once, careful.

The man looked past him at the new studs and fresh boards. He whistled low, almost impressed.

"I sure do hope your new house doesn't catch fire," he said, his tone staying light, almost joking.

Clem didn't smile.

He understood it clean and cold. The house wasn't just a future anymore. It was something a man could burn to prove a point.

That night, Millie moved a little closer to him in bed, and for a moment it felt like the early days, like they were finding each other again. She felt him awake beside her, staring into the dark.

He reached for her hand and held it tight, like he was afraid she'd drift away.

Millie rolled onto her side. His breath warmed her cheek. He kissed her slow, then rested his forehead to hers, and the rest of the night stopped being about money, or walls, or worry.

A month passed, and nothing came.

No word from the helper. No message sent through town. No man riding up with that too-friendly smile. The silence should've felt like relief, but it didn't. It felt like a held breath.

Then Millie's body changed.

At first it was small things. The smell of coffee turning her stomach. The way her appetite went strange, hungry one hour, sick the next. She tried to tell herself it was nerves, that fear could do plenty all on its own. But this nausea had a shape she recognized. It wasn't grief. It was something older, something she'd carried before.

Her cycle ran late. Then later.

Millie didn't need a doctor to know. She sat on the edge of the bed one morning, one hand on her stomach, and the room tilted, not from sickness, but from the weight of the truth.

Pregnant again.

Hope rushed in first, bright and reckless, then fear slammed right into it. She felt guilt, too, sharp as a thorn. Guilt for wanting it after losing John. Guilt for being afraid of it now. And under everything, the terror of losing again, of watching Clem's face go blank, of hearing silence where there should've been a cry.

She told him in the kitchen, with the house frame visible through the window like a promise trying to become real.

Clem just stared at her.

"What?" he said, like the word didn't fit in his mouth.

"I'm pregnant," she repeated, and her voice shook once.

For a second his eyes went wide, stunned and helpless. Then his face hardened into something protective. He stepped closer, like he could block the world with his body.

Millie waited for joy. It tried to show up, but it came in quiet, cautious, like it didn't trust the room.

Clem's hand found her arm. His thumb rubbed the same spot, over and over.

"We'll be careful," he said. "We'll do everything right."

But Millie saw the shadow behind his eyes. He was thinking of the helper. He was thinking of the road. He was thinking of what could arrive without warning.

"This baby deserves a real home," Millie said, and she nodded toward the rising frame outside. "Not a borrowed corner. Not a place that shakes in the wind."

Clem swallowed. The word baby seemed to land inside him like a stone.

Millie watched him closely. His throat worked, and his eyes went far away for a second, like he'd seen the road ahead and didn't like what was on it. His hand stayed on her arm, protective, but his face tightened, like worry had just found a new place to live.

That afternoon he drove himself harder. The next day, too.

He dug in deep, determined, and almost desperate in it.

If there was time left, he was going to turn it into something solid.

He was going to finish that house before the baby came.

Months later, the house stood finished enough to feel real.

Over thirty-five thousand dollars, give or take, turned into studs and siding, glass and shingles, a stove that held heat, walls that didn't rattle when the wind got mean. Even a washing machine. A real structure planted on Montana dirt like it had always belonged there.

Millie walked through it slow. She ran her fingers along the new trim, pressed her palm to the wall in what would be the nursery, and let herself picture it. A table with room for more than two plates. A hallway that didn't end in draft. A life that didn't feel borrowed.

For one clean moment, she felt something like peace.

Clem stood in the doorway watching her, pride in his face, but it didn't reach his eyes. He looked like a man who'd crossed a finish line and found nothing waiting but the next bill.

Because the helper still hadn't been paid.

That afternoon, Clem saw the strange neighbor again, sitting easy at the gate like he'd been there awhile. He didn't wave. He didn't smile.

He just said, "You're out of time."

Clem's stomach went cold.

As the rider turned his horse, Clem understood it plain.

The unpaid favor wasn't a favor anymore.

It was leverage.

CHAPTER ELEVEN

DEBT SETTLED IN FULL

Morning settled into the new house like it belonged there. The boards were still clean, the corners still held a little sawdust, and the place smelled like fresh lumber and work. Millie stood at the sink and let herself take it in, just for a second. A real roof. Real walls. A stove that did not wobble.

The relief didn't last.

Hoofbeats came up the drive, steady and unhurried. Millie looked out through the front window and saw him ride in as if he'd been invited. He swung down easy, straightened his hat, and walked up to the porch with a smile that didn't reach his eyes.

Clem was already moving. He stepped outside before the man could knock, like he'd been waiting for this.

Millie stayed inside, hands braced on the counter. She couldn't make out much, just the low murmur of two men keeping their voices controlled. The helper's posture stayed loose, almost friendly. Clem didn't give him an inch, but Millie saw his shoulders tighten, saw his jaw lock.

She edged toward the doorframe, careful not to let the screen squeak. A few words carried through.

"...twelve-five," the helper said, like he was stating the weather.

Clem's reply came quieter, rougher.

"The cash is gone."

The helper's smile didn't disappear, it just got narrower. His eyes stayed bright, but the friendliness drained out of his voice.

Clem spoke steady. Millie caught enough to understand the shape of it. He wasn't denying anything. He was admitting it.

"I used it," Clem said. "On the house. For my family."

The helper let out a small breath through his nose, almost a laugh, but not quite. He shifted his weight, slow, like he had all day. Then he leaned closer, keeping his voice low. Millie couldn't hear every word, but she caught the ones that landed hard.

"Fire," the helper said.

A pause.

"Insurance," he added, like it was part of a list.

Millie's stomach tightened. Her fingers curled around the edge of the doorframe until her knuckles went pale. She'd never heard a threat delivered so calmly.

Clem didn't step back. He held his ground, shoulders squared. When he answered, his voice stayed even, but it sharpened.

"I can't hand you money I don't have," Clem said. "But I can give you something else."

The helper tipped his head. "Like what?"

Clem took half a step closer, forcing the helper to look at him straight. He spoke quieter, like this was business, not begging.

"One run," Clem said. "Quick. Clean. Worth more than cash. You do it, and you're set. You'll have what you came for, and then some."

The helper watched him, measuring. Millie felt her anger rise, hot and helpless. A run. A favor. Whatever Clem was offering, it sounded like a bargain made with someone else's safety.

The helper's mouth twitched, interested now. "And you think I'd trust that?"

Clem didn't answer right away.

Millie shifted, a board creaking under her heel. Clem's head snapped up.

Their eyes met through the gap of the door.

And in Clem's face, Millie saw something she hadn't seen in a long time. Not fear. Not pleading.

Something like calculation.

Something like a plan.

The same man she'd seen in that courthouse hallway, when he asked her to marry him as if it were the only move left on the board.

Clem and the helper drifted away from the porch, slow, like they were just stretching their legs. They headed toward the fence line where the yard fell off into open ground. Far enough that Millie couldn't catch the words anymore, even with the door cracked and her ear turned.

She watched from the window.

The helper talked with his hands now, pointing once toward the road, then toward the barn, like he was laying out steps. Clem stayed still. He asked questions, one after another, calm and patient. The helper answered fast at first, then started shrugging more, waving things off. Millie couldn't hear what they were saying, but she could see when the helper got irritated. His shoulders rose. His jaw worked. Clem didn't match his heat. He kept pressing with the same steady rhythm, forcing the answers to tighten.

Then Clem reached into his shirt pocket and pulled out a small folded paper and a stub of pencil.

Millie leaned closer to the glass.

Clem flattened the paper against the top rail of the fence and wrote on it, quick and controlled. He held it out. The helper looked down, hesitated just long enough to show it mattered, then took the pencil and added his name.

Millie watched the exchange from a distance and felt a chill she couldn't explain. It was the way Clem held the pencil out, the way he waited, patient and sure, like the signing was the whole point. It looked too familiar.

Exactly like he'd done with her years earlier.

Millie's grip tightened on the window frame. She couldn't tell which scared her more, that Clem was being reckless, or that he might be brilliant.

Clem read the paper once, folded it, and slipped it back into his pocket without a flicker. The helper's posture loosened. He stuck out his hand.

Clem took it.

They shook once, firm, then let go.

Millie's stomach flipped. She didn't like that handshake; the moment their palms touched, it stopped looking like men talking and started looking like a deal.

* * *

WHEN CLEM CAME BACK to the porch, his face was set. Not angry, not scared, just decided. He stepped inside and shut the door behind him, quiet, like he didn't want the helper hearing the click.

Millie didn't wait. "What did he want?"

Clem glanced toward the window, then back at her. "He wants me to run cattle through," he said. "Under my name."

Millie stared at him. "Cattle from where?"

"That's the part he wouldn't say," Clem answered. "No clear papers. No clean origin. He kept calling it 'mostly paperwork,' like that makes it harmless."

Millie felt her anger come up sharp. "So he's using you."

Clem nodded once. "He thinks my name makes it sell." Clem's voice stayed level. "I told him I'd do it, but only on my conditions."

* * *

MILLIE DIDN'T SPEAK RIGHT AWAY. She watched Clem's face, waiting for him to dress it up, to soften it. He didn't.

"What conditions?" she asked.

Clem reached into his pocket and pulled out the folded paper. He didn't hand it to her yet. He just held it, like the weight of it mattered.

"A document," he said. "Simple. Handwritten. Signed."

Millie's eyes dropped to the paper.

"It says, 'Debt settled in full,'" Clem told her. "Dated today. My name, his name. That's it."

Millie blinked. "He signed that?"

"He laughed," Clem said. "Called it pointless." His mouth tightened a fraction. "Then he signed anyway, because he thinks it doesn't hurt him."

Millie felt a cold line run through her chest. "And you let him."

Clem looked at her then, steady. "I needed him to."

"You're at it again," she said. Her voice stayed low, but it wasn't gentle. "You are putting us in danger."

Clem didn't argue. He set his hat on the table like he needed his hands free, then looked at her straight. "I know what I'm doing."

"That's what you said before," Millie shot back. "And before that." She pointed toward the window, toward the fence line where the deal had been made. "You make it sound simple, and then the ground shifts under us."

Clem sat up straight, not from anger, from restraint. "I'm not laying it all out," he said. "Not because I don't want you to know, because the less you can truthfully say, the better."

Millie held his eyes. "So I'm supposed to just stand here and hope you're right."

Clem's voice stayed level. "You're supposed to trust me."

The words hit an old place in her. Millie saw that courthouse hallway again, Clem stepping in close, speaking like a man who'd already decided the only way forward. She hadn't trusted him then because she felt safe. She trusted him because she'd read the world, and she'd read him. She'd known he had a plan.

Millie took a breath. "Fine. I'll trust you." Her tone sharpened. "But I want one thing."

Clem waited.

"No surprises," she said. "And no illegal mess that costs us this ranch. Not after everything we've put into it."

Clem nodded once. "Agreed."

Millie didn't move, didn't let him off easy. "Say it."

Clem's eyes didn't flinch. "I'm not dirtying our name," he said. "I'm cleaning this up."

Millie still didn't like it. She still felt the edge of fear under her ribs.

But she stepped closer anyway, and stood beside him like that was her decision too.

They prepared to leave before full daylight. The truck hummed over cold ruts while Millie kept one hand on her belly and the other on the dash."

The auction yard was already waking up when they pulled in. Trailers backed in slow. Men leaned on gates with coffee cups. Voices carried, easy and sharp, like everyone knew everyone, and everyone knew what had happened last time Clem showed up.

Clem spotted the rig he was looking for, a heavy hauler parked near the back shadows, mud-caked and quiet. He told Millie to wait. He walked over, casual but quick, and shone a penlight through the slats of the trailer.

The beam caught hide and hair. He traced the brand on the nearest steer. It was altered, crude work that wouldn't pass a second look, and it definitely didn't match the papers in his pocket.

He clicked the light off, satisfied. The trap was set.

Millie felt the shift in him the moment he stepped back

toward her. Heads turned. A few nods followed him. Not friendly, not rude, more like attention.

Clem didn't act proud. He acted careful.

The helper was there too, pretending it was just another morning, but Millie saw the tightness in his mouth when Clem walked straight past the office and toward the pens.

Clem spoke to the barn hands like he belonged there. "We do this clean," he said. "In daylight."

The helper tried to slide in close. He murmured something, quick and annoyed.

Clem didn't look at him. He raised his voice just enough for the nearest men to hear. "I won't move cattle without a brand check."

A couple of the hands paused. One of them glanced toward the office.

The helper's smile flashed and died. "Clem, we don't need all that," he said, too smooth. "It's fine. Let's keep it moving."

Clem stayed calm. "Brand check first."

He made it sound routine, like this was how he always worked. Millie didn't hear him accuse or threaten. He just insisted.

The barn manager came over, wiping his hands on his jeans, curious but not alarmed. Clem spoke with him a moment, quiet, controlled. Then the manager nodded and called for the iron to be turned and the first animal to be brought up.

Millie stood at the rail, the smell of cattle and dust thick in her nose. Her heart kicked once when the first cow was pushed into place and turned enough for the mark to show.

The voices around her shifted.

Not loud, not panicked, but sharp with interest.

Something was wrong. Millie could see it in the way the brand didn't sit right, in the way the barn hand hesitated before he said a word.

And because Clem had demanded the check, right here, right now, in front of everybody, Millie realized what he'd done.

Whatever this was, it wasn't going to land on him.

Men started looking at Clem like he'd just proven something all over again, and Millie hated how steady he looked while her stomach stayed tight.

The cow shifted in the alley, hooves scraping plank, and the barn hand turned her just enough for the mark to show clear.

The inspector leaned in, eyes narrowed. He didn't say much at first. He didn't have to. His hand hovered near the hide, tracing the shape without touching. Then he looked down at the papers.

Millie watched the pause lengthen.

The barn didn't go silent all at once. It quieted in pieces. A laugh stopped. A gate chain quit rattling. Someone cleared his throat and didn't follow it with a joke.

The inspector spoke to the manager, low, then pointed again. The manager's posture changed. His face lost that easy, morning look. He took the papers and held them closer, then looked at the animal like he was seeing it for the first time.

Millie heard a man behind her murmur, "That ain't right."

The inspector called out one detail, then another, like he was building a list. Brand didn't match. Earmark was off. Something had been cut or altered, enough to make a clean story impossible.

Clem didn't rush in. He stepped back from the rail, one full pace, then another, creating space between himself and the cow. His hands stayed where everyone could see them. When he spoke, his voice carried, controlled.

"I'm seeing it now," Clem said. "Same as you."

The helper moved fast, trying to slide in front of it all. He laughed it off as a mix-up, like everybody should relax. He clapped the manager on the shoulder as if they were friends. He started talking about mistakes, bad ink, tired eyes.

No one laughed with him.

Clem held his ground. "I won't move cattle without a brand

inspection," he said, steady and loud enough that men two pens away could hear. "Daylight. In front of witnesses."

Millie felt the shift. The eyes that had been on Clem swung away from him and landed on the helper. Not curiosity anymore, not gossip. Measurement.

The helper tried to pull Clem aside. He caught Clem's sleeve and leaned in, mouth close to his ear.

Clem didn't go with him. He didn't yank away either. He just stood there and made the helper do it in the open.

Millie couldn't hear the words, but she saw the helper's jaw working, saw the tight edge of his smile. He was pressing. He was warning. But he couldn't raise his voice. He couldn't shove. Every move he made drew more attention.

The manager took control. He lifted a hand and called for the lot to be held. He asked for the paperwork again. He asked for names. He asked who hauled the cattle, who signed the entry, who claimed ownership.

The helper started backing up, changing his story in small steps. He talked faster. He offered half answers and tried to sound insulted. It didn't work. The inspector stayed calm and kept pointing to what didn't line up.

Then the manager stepped away and spoke to someone Millie couldn't see. A few minutes later, a man in a hat came through the side gate, not in a hurry, but direct.

The sheriff.

Millie's heart hammered as the helper tried one last smile, one last joke, and the sheriff didn't take it. He asked him to come with him, and this time the helper couldn't pretend it was nothing.

Millie watched Clem from the rail, his face still, his shoulders square. And she understood it plain.

What Clem had set up clicked into place, right in front of everybody.

Clem didn't linger.

When the sheriff led the helper away, the barn started

breathing again, slow and uneasy. Men went back to their coffee. Gates clanked. Somebody made a joke that fell flat. The work tried to return to normal, but the air stayed changed.

Clem spoke once more with the manager and the inspector. Millie watched him nod, watched him keep his hands quiet, watched him say as little as possible. When it was done, he walked out with the folded paper in his pocket, the one the helper had signed like it meant nothing.

Behind them, the helper's face flashed through the railings, red and sharp with rage. He didn't shout. He couldn't. Not now. Every eye in the place knew where the trouble had started, and if he reached for Clem, he'd only drag himself deeper.

The sheriff didn't look satisfied. He asked questions that didn't stop at this one lot. He spoke to the manager again, then to the inspector, and Millie could tell it wasn't ending at the auction barn. Not for the helper.

On the drive home, the truck cab stayed quiet. The road rolled under them, familiar and empty, but Millie's body still felt the barn, the moment when the crowd turned, the moment the sheriff appeared. Relief sat in her chest, but it didn't settle. It kept bumping against something else.

Finally, Millie said it, the truth in one breath. "I'm proud of you, and I'm mad at you, and I'm scared."

Clem kept his eyes on the road. His voice came calm, final. "It's done," he said. "The debt is paid."

CHAPTER TWELVE

GOODBYE WORK

The house wasn't finished, not the way a proper home was supposed to be finished. One window still stuck. The back steps were temporary boards Clem promised he'd "make right." The trim in the front room sat stacked against the wall, waiting on time they didn't have.

Still, it had a roof that didn't leak, a stove that worked, and a door that latched.

Millie stood in the middle of the main room with both hands on her belly and let herself take it in. Big pregnant now, pregnant enough that every chore felt like two chores. Moving in felt like family. It felt real.

They carried in what they had. A quilt. A box of dishes. Some groceries. Then a tightness grabbed low in her belly, and she had to sit down.

The first pain hit low and clean, and Millie knew what it was. Not sickness, not strain, not the ordinary aches she'd been carrying for months. This was labor, and it didn't ask permission.

Clem was at her side before she said his name. His face went tight for a second, then he moved, steady and quick. He called the midwife and got everything settled before she showed up.

The midwife arrived with cold hands and a calm voice. She checked Millie, nodded, and told her what to do next, steady and practiced, like reading from a list she'd memorized years ago.

The hours blurred. Pain rose, broke, and came again. Millie held on to Clem's hand and the edge of the bed and the sound of the midwife counting. Between contractions, she watched Clem. He wasn't the same as last time. He didn't pace. He didn't talk too much. He stayed close, like he'd learned where to put his fear.

The room changed. The pressure shifted, the midwife leaned in, and Millie bore down until her body gave up what it had been holding.

A cry filled the space, sharp and alive.

The midwife looked up, smiling. "What do we name him?"

Him. The word landed soft and right.

Clem swallowed and said it like he'd been carrying it a long time. "William."

Millie managed a wet laugh, half relief, half disbelief. "William," she repeated, and the name settled in the room like it belonged there.

The midwife laid him against her, warm and slick and breathing, and Millie held on as if she could keep the world from taking anything else.

With the helper in prison, the house got quieter in a way Millie didn't know she'd been missing. She still locked the door at night, still listened for tires on the road, but the fear wasn't sitting in her throat anymore. It eased back, little by little, until she could look out the window without bracing for something.

Clem fell into a routine that made sense to him. He was up before light, coffee strong, boots on, moving like he didn't know how to be still. Millie learned the rhythm too, even with a baby on her hip. Feed first. Water. Fence checks. Then whatever the day decided to throw at them.

Word traveled, the way it always did. Folks talked about the barn, the brands, the sheriff showing up. They talked about Clem keeping his head and walking out with his paper signed. At first, Millie hated hearing it repeated. Then she saw what it did. Buyers didn't lean in and test him as hard. Men who liked to cut corners didn't push so close. Clem's name carried weight now, and the ranch benefitted from it.

The midwife lived on a neighboring farm, not close enough to be called neighbors, but close enough to show up when it mattered. She had a little girl named Maria, three or four at the time William was born. Maria came around with her mother at first, then came on her own. At first, her mother sent her with small errands. Then Maria started making up errands just to have a reason to come and see Millie and the baby. She had quick hands and a serious face, and she watched everything like she meant to remember it.

Millie found her in the kitchen one morning, standing on a chair to reach the counter, trying to peel a potato with more confidence than skill. Millie should've scolded her. Instead, she handed her a duller knife and stayed nearby.

After that, Maria was just there. She carried kindling. She gathered eggs. She made herself useful without being asked, like she was practicing for a life she planned to earn. When William got old enough to sit up and grab at anything within reach, Maria hovered close, talking to him like he understood every word.

It happened slowly, then all at once. Millie realized she trusted Maria. Trusted her to hold William while Millie hauled water. Trusted her to keep him shaded while Millie worked the garden rows. Trusted her enough to leave the room and not feel that hard panic rise.

Some days, Millie looked up and saw Clem with Maria at his heel and William in his arms, and it hit her that their little family was bigger than three. The ranch was still hard. The work still demanded everything. But now it felt like they were building something that could last.

* * *

MILLIE SET everything out that William might need. Then she handed him to Maria. Maria took him with an ease that settled Millie some, lifting him to her hip and keeping one arm firm around his middle. "I'll keep him close," Maria promised, serious as a grown woman. Millie was still nervous, but she rode out anyway, telling herself she could get the work done, then be back before supper.

The cattle move started like the others. Dust, boots, the steady push of bodies up the draw. Millie rode a little behind Clem, keeping the line tight, watching for the small problems before they became big ones.

The sky changed while they worked. Not all at once, but enough that Millie noticed. The light went flat. The wind shifted and stayed shifted. A cool edge slipped under her shirt.

She looked west and didn't like what she saw.

"Clem," she called.

He glanced back, calm as ever. "We're fine," he said. "Stay put."

The herd picked up on it before any human did. Heads lifted. Tails flicked. A few cows started to crowd, pressing shoulder to shoulder like they wanted to be anywhere else.

Thunder sounded far off, then closer, like it had decided.

Millie's hands tightened on the reins. She could turn back now, take the long way, get ahead of trouble. Or she could do what Clem asked and trust him to hold the line.

She stayed where she was, but it wasn't easy. It wasn't obedience either. It was a choice she didn't like making.

The fence gave with a sound Millie felt more than heard. A sharp crack, then the wire sang loose. One post leaned, then snapped at the base like it had been cut. The gap opened just wide enough, then widened again as the strain hit it.

The first cow shoved through. The rest followed like they'd been waiting.

Clem rode hard to the break, angling his horse to turn them back. He shouted, low and firm, trying to push the lead cows sideways, trying to make the herd bend instead of bolt. For a moment, it almost worked.

Then the wind slapped rain into Millie's face and the world went gray. The ground turned slick under hoof. Mud sucked at everything moving.

The herd surged again. It wasn't a few head now, it was a wall of bodies and fear, pressing through the gap and widening it with every shove. Clem disappeared behind them, then showed again, then vanished. Millie couldn't tell where the fence ended and the cattle began.

"Clem!" she yelled, and her voice sounded small against the thunder.

He lifted an arm, a signal she couldn't read, and drove in closer, trying to get ahead of the lead cows. His horse slipped. Clem jerked the reins, recovered, and kept going like it didn't matter.

It mattered.

A cow spun, blind with panic, and slammed the line. Another followed. Clem's horse took a hit to the shoulder and stumbled. Clem leaned, trying to stay in the saddle, trying to keep his body out of the crush.

Millie broke her position and shoved her horse in, hooves sliding in the wet ground, reins tight in her fists. She shouted until her throat burned. The rain swallowed the sound.

She saw it then, clear and wrong. Clem went down. Not a fall you got up from laughing, not a fall you walked off. He hit the mud hard, and the horse rolled away, scrambling, eyes wide.

Millie reached him, threw herself off the saddle, and hit the mud on her knees.

His face was turned toward her, but his focus wasn't. His breaths were thin and spaced out, like his body was rationing them.

Millie touched his shoulder and knew, with a cold certainty, this wasn't hurt.

This was ending.

Millie didn't remember deciding to move. She was just moving.

Her hands went under Clem's shoulders. Mud slicked her palms, his coat, her sleeves. He was heavy in a way that scared her, heavy like a man who wasn't helping his own body anymore.

There were men with them on the move, hired hands and a neighbor who'd come for the day. Millie snapped her head up. "Get the truck," she shouted, and when no one moved fast enough, she pointed at a boy on a horse. "You. Now. Ride. Tell them to bring it to the gate."

A couple of men came in close. One hesitated, eyes on the herd still milling and snorting in the rain.

"Leave the cattle," Millie snapped. "If you want to be useful, put your hands on him."

They lifted Clem together, awkward and careful. He made a sound through his teeth, then went quiet. Millie kept talking because silence felt like permission for the world to stop.

"Easy," she told them. "Feet first. Watch the rut. Don't let his head drop."

Clem's eyes opened, then slid away. He came back for a second, found her face.

"Millie," he said, and his voice was thin but steady.

"I'm here."

His fingers caught her wrist, not strong, but deliberate. Like he needed her to understand.

"Don't," he whispered.

"Don't what?"

He swallowed, and for a moment she thought he'd slipped away again. Then he pulled air and said it clearer, each word placed.

"Don't waste time."

The truck finally lurched into view, tires spinning, men jumping down.

Millie made herself stand.

She wasn't doing rescue work anymore. She felt that truth settle in her chest like a weight.

This was goodbye work, and it was going to be done right.

They got him to the house, not gentle, just careful. Maria's mom was already there when they came through the door, apron thrown on over whatever she'd been doing. She checked him once, then again, and her face told Millie more than any words could.

Millie sat close enough to feel Clem's breath when it came. His skin had gone damp and cool. His eyes opened, closed, opened again, like he had to spend effort just to stay with her.

He found her hand and held on.

"You did it," he said.

Millie leaned in. "Did what?"

He swallowed. "You changed me. You taught me love. You made me better. I wasn't this man before you."

Millie stared at him, waiting, because she could tell he wasn't finished. His thumb moved once over her knuckles, slow, deliberate.

"There was a girl after the war," he said. "Back East. I thought I was done with everything, but I wasn't. She told me she was pregnant."

Millie felt the words hit, sharp and clean. She didn't pull her hand away.

"I ran," Clem said. "I didn't check. I didn't go back. I just left. I told myself it wasn't mine. That I didn't owe her anything. But I knew what I was doing. I was scared, and I was selfish."

Millie wanted to cry. Anger rose, then hurt, then something worse, the thought of all the years he'd carried it alone while she had built a life beside him.

"I wanted to tell you," he said. "So many times. Then we had

John. Then we lost him. Then we had William. I kept thinking, not now. Not ever. I didn't want you to look at me and see that."

Millie blinked hard. Her voice came steady, even if her body wasn't.

"I see you," she said.

His eyes fixed on her face like it was the last thing he needed to keep.

Millie squeezed his hand and leaned closer. "You're here," she told him. "You stayed. You fought for us. I'm not letting you go alone."

Clem exhaled, long and thin. His fingers tightened once, then eased.

Millie pressed her forehead to his hand for one second, just to borrow strength, then lifted her head and stayed with him.

He looked at her, held her gaze, and then his eyes went still.

CHAPTER THIRTEEN

DEBT DOESN'T DIE

The rain finally quit, but the ranch didn't look relieved.

Mud held every bootprint. Wire hung loose where the fence had snapped. A few boards lay flat like they'd been slapped down. Cows stood bunched in the low ground, sides heaving, blinking at the world.

Millie didn't let herself think about the sky. She kept her eyes on what still needed doing.

Clem lay on the floor where they'd gotten him in before the wind turned mean again. The room still smelled like wet wool and storm, and the boards under him held the weight of what had happened.

Millie didn't say his name. She couldn't risk her voice breaking open. She took a sheet from the shelf, unfolded it with hands that didn't feel like hers, and covered him from boots to shoulders. She stopped at his face, swallowed once, then pulled the sheet the last few inches and turned her head away. The gesture felt final, and it made her chest tighten hard.

His eyes had gone still, and the stillness stayed.

She stood there one more second, listening for a sound she

already knew wouldn't come, then she forced her feet to move. She didn't let herself sit. If she sat, she might not get up.

Water chores still needed to be done. Always water. The troughs didn't care what had happened, and the animals didn't get a day off. Millie stepped out into the mud, pulled her coat tight, and went straight to the pump.

She checked the trough line first. The windmill still turned, slow and stubborn. The pump handle fought her, then gave. Water ran brown at first, then cleared. She watched it a beat longer than necessary, like the sound could keep her standing.

Then she moved.

She rode to the nearest place with smoke in the chimney. A woman she'd spoken to twice, maybe three times, met her at the gate, hands red from cold, eyes sharp with questions.

"Something's gone bad at my place," Millie said. "I need you to send for the sheriff."

The neighbor just nodded.

The sheriff came. Not fast, not slow, just like he'd seen this kind of thing before. He took his hat off when he saw the sheet. He asked a few questions that felt like stones. Millie answered them anyway. Where? When? How long? Did he speak? Did he suffer? She kept her words plain. She didn't decorate the truth. The land didn't need help being cruel.

They buried Clem two days later, on the ridge where the ground stayed firm. No preacher. No speeches. A few neighbors came with hats in their hands and eyes that wouldn't settle anywhere. Someone brought a shovel. Someone brought coffee in a tin. They stayed long enough to finish the work, then they drifted back to their lives, because their cows still needed hay and their fences still needed wire.

Millie went back to the new house when it was over.

It hit harder than the burial.

The rooms were bigger than they had any right to be. The table had four chairs, but only one felt real now. William played on the floor while Maria sat close, older by a few years and always underfoot. And it made her throat burn.

She stood in the doorway and looked out over the land Clem had bled for.

Her knees shook. Her hands did too.

Then she turned away from the view, stepped inside, and chose the living anyway.

Eight months after the storm, seasons turned. Time kept moving. Work kept showing up.

Millie was at the table with a pencil and a stack of paper, doing what she always did now, making numbers behave. The stove ticked. The house held quiet the way it did when you learned not to waste sound.

A knock came, sharp and certain.

She didn't jump, but her spine tightened. Nobody knocked like that unless they expected the door to open.

Millie wiped her hands on her skirt, even though they weren't dirty, and crossed the room. She opened the door and found him on the steps.

The Helper.

He looked the same, like time hadn't bothered teaching him manners. His hat sat low. His eyes stayed flat.

"No condolences?" Millie asked.

He gave a small shrug, like her grief wasn't on his list.

"I'm not here for that," he said. "I'm here because the deal's still the deal. I did my time in jail, but the debt didn't sit in that cell with me. It was waiting right here."

Millie didn't step back. She kept her body in the doorway, blocking the warm air, blocking the house.

"Clem's gone," she said, blocking the doorway.

"And the debt's not." He picked at a splinter on the rail, bored. "Eight months. That's what you got."

"He had you sign a release," Millie said. "Debt paid."

The Helper's mouth twitched. "Paper's for men who still care about paper."

She felt the words land clean and cold. So this was it. Not mercy, not patience, just a leash he'd chosen to loosen.

"How much?" she asked.

He named it, and it wasn't a number meant to be paid by a woman alone. He watched her face like he wanted to see her break.

Millie didn't give him that.

"If you can't pay," he said, leaning in just enough to make it a warning, "you'll lose more than money. Folks misplace things out here. Papers. Stock. Equipment. Things catch on fire."

Millie held his stare and let the threat sit in her chest without showing it.

"Message received," she said.

Behind her, the floorboard gave a soft creak.

Millie didn't turn, but she knew. Maria had slipped behind the door, listening with her whole little body.

The Helper's mouth twitched, like he'd noticed too.

Then he tipped his hat once, not polite, just final, and walked off the porch as if he owned the road away. He stopped and turned, "I'll be back soon. Have my money or you'll pay another way."

Millie waited until the Helper was out of sight and down the road before she moved.

Maria stood in the hallway, pale and quiet, her small hands clenched at her sides like she was holding herself together.

Millie crouched in front of her. "Tell me what you heard," she said, soft but steady.

Maria swallowed. "He said you'd lose more than money," she whispered. "He said things could burn."

Millie nodded. "All right." She kissed Maria's forehead and sent her to the back room with a picture book. Then she went to the phone and cranked the handle until the line caught.

"Operator," a woman said, brisk and tired.

"It's Millie Spyker," Millie told her. "Get me the sheriff."

The pause felt too long. Millie heard a faint murmur in the background, then a soft click as the connection shifted.

The sheriff answered like he already knew trouble lived out here.

Millie told him everything, word for word, no extra. She gave him the time, the tone, the threat. She told him Maria heard it too.

"I'm coming now," the sheriff said.

Millie shut her eyes for half a second. Relief tried to show up. She didn't let it stay.

"How long?" she asked.

"Soon as I can get there," he said. "Keep the door locked. Don't let him in. Keep your girl close."

"All right," Millie said.

"I'll need your statement," he added. "And Maria's. I'll write it down, proper. I'll log the threat. Then I'll go find him and make it clear he's on notice."

Millie listened, breathing slow, holding herself quiet.

"You do that," she said.

"I will," he answered, and she heard the hard edge behind it. "Stay where you are. I'll see you when I get there."

He hung up.

Millie didn't move for a second. She set the receiver down like it might break if she didn't.

Just over an hour later, the sheriff's truck rolled into the yard, tires crunching. He stepped out with his hat low and his coat buttoned up, a man who didn't waste words when weather and trouble were both on the ground.

He took his hat off at the threshold. "Mrs. Spyker."

Millie opened the door wider and let him in. "Sheriff."

He looked at her face, then past her shoulder toward the hallway, toward the back of the house.

"Tell me exactly what he said," he told her, voice steady, pen already out. "Start at the beginning."

Millie repeated it straight through, no softening, no guessing. Time. Tone. The words that mattered. She watched his pen move, fast and neat, like he was trying to get ahead of what could happen next.

He asked to speak with Maria.

Millie brought her to the kitchen table, one hand resting on the girl's shoulder. Maria's eyes were wide, but she didn't flinch.

"Did you hear him say anything?" the sheriff asked.

Maria nodded. "Yes, sir."

"Tell me what you heard."

Maria said it the same way Millie had, small voice, stubborn truth. Papers. Cows. Fire.

The sheriff didn't write for a second. He took a slow breath, like he was setting something down inside himself, then he looked Millie in the eye.

"I want you to understand the problem," he said. "Town's a drive. By the time I get there, whatever he's come to do, he might already have done it."

Millie stared at the wall behind him, jaw tight enough to ache. When she spoke, her voice didn't rise.

"So what do I do?"

There was a pause. Not hesitation, just weight.

"Legally," he said, "you don't have to let someone force their way into your home. If you're in danger, you can protect yourself. You hear me?"

"I hear you."

"Good," he said, quieter still. "If it comes to that, I'll have your back. Maria's statement helps. It's on record now."

Millie nodded. She understood.

That afternoon, she drove to the feed store and bought a shotgun and a box of shells. The man behind the counter didn't ask why. He just showed her how it worked. Millie listened like her life depended on it, because it did.

By the next day, she knew how to load it, how to hold it, how to make it fire. She even tested it on a few boards behind the barn. The boards did not survive.

Later that week, the pounding started before dawn.

The Helper hit the door again and again, hard enough to rattle the frame. Millie stood in the dark with the gun braced in both hands, Maria behind her, silent and shaking.

The door gave. The Helper shoved in.

Millie fired once, low and steady, like she'd practiced.

The Helper went down hard, and the house swallowed the sound.

When the Sheriff's headlights finally swept the yard, he found the door shattered and the body on the floor. He didn't even unholster his weapon. He stepped over the debris, checked the Helper, and looked at Millie.

"You filed the report," he said, his voice grim but settled. "You called it in before he ever touched that latch. That call is the difference between a crime scene and a closed case."

He looked at the splinters of the broken doorframe. "Forcible entry. Documented threat. This is clear-cut self-defense, Millie. We'll need a statement tomorrow, but tonight, you stay here."

Millie shook so hard her teeth clicked. She cried without meaning to. She prayed out loud.

Then she ran outside and vomited in the yard.

After the Sheriff left, she looked back at the room where William slept. The fear was still there, but it didn't get to her like before.

She had come too far to let anyone take it from her.

CHAPTER FOURTEEN

BUCKLE AND BLOODLINE

Millie didn't call it raising a boy.

She called it building someone who could stand.

The first weeks after the Helper went down, she moved like she was carrying glass inside her chest. She still did chores. She still cooked. She still checked the fence line and the latch and the windows before she slept. But the sound of that shot stayed in her ears, and some nights she woke up nervous.

William slept through most of it. He was too young to know what he'd almost lost.

Millie knew.

That was enough.

She stopped waiting for the world to be fair. She stopped hoping men would "do right" because it was right. Hope was fine for church. Out here it needed a spine.

So she gave it one.

She made rules and she kept them. The ranch ran on work, and it ran on truth, and it ran on prayer said with your hands busy.

When William was big enough to follow her without tripping,

she let him come. Not into danger. Not into trouble. Just into the day.

She showed him cattle first, because cattle were honest. They didn't lie, and they didn't apologize.

"See the ears?" she'd tell him, pointing without jabbing. "See the tail? See how they're standing? That's them talking."

He'd squint like he could force the meaning out of it.

"Don't go behind one you don't know," she'd say. "And don't stand where you can't move."

She taught him how to move slow around animals, how to step out of pressure instead of fighting it, how to keep his voice steady even when he felt jumpy.

When he got older, she taught him wire. Not pretty lessons, but real ones. "Gloves," she said, and made him put them on. "You only forget once."

She showed him how to staple right, how to pull without snapping the line, how to check corners because corners were where things failed first. When he wanted to rush, she made him redo it.

"Fast breaks," she'd tell him. "Straight holds."

Then it was the weather. She didn't teach him by reading a newspaper, but by making him look up. "Feel that?" she'd ask when the air went thin and sharp. "That's a change coming."

She taught him to watch clouds for shape and speed, to smell rain before it arrived, to notice when birds got quiet. She never treated it as magic. It was attention, the kind that saved your life when nobody was coming to save it for you.

Horses came last, and only when she was sure he wouldn't get brave in the wrong way.

"Brave is fine," she told him. "Stupid will put you in the ground."

William wanted to ride like the men he'd seen from the road, loose and loud, like the horse was a toy. Millie didn't raise toys.

She made him brush first, feed first, check hooves first. She made him learn where a horse's fear lived, and what it looked like before it turned into a kick. When he got bucked off once, he sat there in the dirt, shocked and embarrassed.

Millie didn't laugh.

She walked up, checked him quick, then said, "All right. Now you decide. You get back on, or you go home and tell yourself a story about why you couldn't."

William stared at her like she'd slapped him with words.

Then he got back on.

That was when she started calling him Spike.

Not as a cute nickname. Not as a joke.

He'd come out of a tumble with a scraped elbow and a stubborn glare, and something about it hit her like recognition. Sharp. Hard to move. Hard to bend.

"You're a Spike," she said.

William blinked. "Like a nail?"

"No, not a nail," she said, smiling. "Like your daddy was. I've got something to show you later."

The name stuck.

But Millie didn't let it become pride without weight. She didn't let it become a mask.

She took him to the ridge when he was old enough to walk the climb without whining. It became their place, not sacred, not sentimental, just steady. A spot where you could see the whole stretch of land, the creek line, the fence breaks, the work waiting in every direction.

She didn't bring him up there to daydream.

She brought him up there to tell the truth.

"This land costs," she said. "Every day."

She told him about men who smiled while they measured what you had. She told him about papers and deadlines and how a neat signature could be a knife if you didn't read it. She told him not to gamble the land, not with cards and not with pride.

"Don't borrow money unless you understand the risk," she

said. "And don't make secret deals. Secrets are where trouble grows."

William would stare out at the creek like he was trying to see the future in it.

One day he asked her, quiet, "Did somebody try to take it?"

Millie didn't dodge. She never dodged with him.

"Yes," she said. "More than once."

He swallowed. "Did you stop them?"

Millie's hand rested on his shoulder, firm. "I did what I had to do."

She didn't say the word shot. Not yet. Not that day.

She told him about Clem too. The good and the ugly, straight down the middle.

"Your daddy could work," she said. "He could read animals better than most men read letters. He could fix things that didn't want to be fixed."

William's eyes would brighten at that.

Then she'd add, "He also made mistakes. He kept things quiet when he should've spoken. He could go cold when he got scared. And he didn't always know the difference between protecting us and controlling the world."

William would frown, chewing on it.

Millie didn't soften it. She also didn't poison it.

"He loved you," she'd say. "He loved this place. And he tried, even when he did it wrong."

On a late fall afternoon when William was tall enough that his boots looked like they belonged, Millie brought a small wrapped bundle up to the ridge. She'd kept it tucked away, out of sight, out of reach, because some things needed time before they could be carried.

She unwrapped it and held out an old buckle. Worn. Solid. Something you earned by surviving.

"This was your daddy's," she said.

William didn't grab for it. He looked at it like it might be too heavy, even in her hand.

Millie held it steady anyway. "If you wear it, you wear what comes with it."

His throat worked. "What comes with it?"

Millie didn't look away. "Work. Straight dealing. No hiding. You protect what's yours, but you don't become what you hate."

William reached for the buckle then, careful, like he understood it wasn't a toy.

He turned it over in his hands. The metal caught light. His fingers tightened.

Millie watched him, quiet, letting the moment land the way it wanted to land.

William lifted his chin and looked out over the ranch like he was taking a measurement only he could take.

Then he said, low and sure, "I won't let them take it."

She nodded. "Good."

William held the buckle a moment longer, then looked at her. "And Spike?" he asked.

Millie kept her voice calm, because she didn't want him thinking this was about ego. "Spike is a choice," she said. "You earn it every day."

William nodded like he'd already decided.

He slipped the buckle into his pocket, a promise he meant to keep.

Millie stood beside him on the ridge and watched the wind move through grass that still needed tending. The ranch didn't look finished. It never would.

* * *

YEARS MOVED ON WITHOUT ASKING.

Millie watched them stack up the way hay bales did, one season after another. William grew into the work like he'd been made for it. Not loud. Not showy. Just steady. A man people counted on, even when they didn't say it out loud.

He kept the ranch profitable. He learned which costs were worth it, and which ones were just a man trying to feel bigger than his land. He didn't gamble. He didn't chase shiny ideas. He fixed what needed fixing, paid what needed paying, and showed up every morning like the day depended on him.

Because it did.

Millie didn't have to hover anymore. That surprised her most. There came a point where she realized she trusted him without checking her own fear first. She'd still wake up early, still listen to the wind and the boards and the quiet, but the panic that used to ride with her had thinned. It wasn't gone. It just wasn't driving.

Late 1993, William brought Elizabeth Bridges home.

Beth.

Millie could tell right away the girl wasn't pretending. Beth stepped out of the truck and looked around like she wanted to learn every inch of it. No squealing. No fancy talk. She smiled at the pasture, at the barn, at the sky, like she already understood what it meant to love a place that demanded something back.

William looked at her like he'd found the one steady thing he didn't have to fight for.

They married in the barn, simple and warm. A few friends. A few chairs. Clean swept boards and a little string of lights that made the rafters look kinder. Beth wore a plain cotton dress. No sparkle, no fuss. Just her, standing there with her hands folded, cheeks pink from the cold.

A friend showed up with a nice camera. He had William turn toward Beth and just look at her. Not at the lens. At her.

Millie saw it in that second, the way William's face softened, the way Beth's eyes held steady. She knew that photo would matter long after the day was over.

Before the vows, Millie pulled William aside. She didn't make a speech. She didn't need to.

She slipped her silver and turquoise ring into his palm.

"This is for her," she said.

William stared down at it, then up at Millie, like he understood the weight of what she was handing him. He closed his fingers around it.

"I know," he said.

When he gave it to Beth, her eyes filled fast. She tried to blink it back, but Millie saw the gratitude land in her the way good things do, quiet and deep.

Millie made another decision that week, just as plain.

William and Beth would live in the big house.

She didn't start something new. She finished something she'd been working toward. The old shack had been sitting there for years, patched enough to stand, ignored enough to feel like a ghost. Millie had already put money aside, saved boards, made a list.

After the wedding, she and William went at it steady. When they needed to, they hired out the parts that took more hands. A month of early mornings and long evenings, replacing what was rotten, straightening what sagged, tightening up the roof, putting in real windows that faced the western pasture. William built her a small covered porch without making a thing of it, like he'd been waiting for the chance.

In the end, it wasn't fancy. It wasn't fragile.

It was hers. Perfect. She'd started calling it the house she built.

That first evening, she sat on the porch with coffee in hand and watched Beth and William walk the yard together. Beth leaned into him like she belonged there.

Millie let herself breathe.

The ranch had a future. And so did she.

A little over a month after the wedding, Millie went up to the big house and found Beth in the kitchen with both hands on her belly, smiling like she was scared to let it show.

"I'm pregnant," she said.

Millie froze for half a breath, then crossed the room and held her. Just held her, as if her arms could keep the world from turning.

Beth told William that afternoon. Millie saw it from the yard, the way his whole face changed when Beth spoke. He lifted her off the ground and laughed, then set her down gentle, like she was made of something holy.

He went right back to work.

That was William.

Later, he came in with dust on his shirt and along the creases of his hands. He rinsed at the pump and paused, sniffing once, uneasy.

"That doesn't smell like dust," he muttered.

Beth asked what he meant.

William shrugged and kissed her forehead. "Probably nothing."

That night he sat at the table with his shoulders hunched, staring at his plate like he couldn't remember why it was there. He said he felt cold. Then hot. Then cold again. His joints ached. He coughed, dry and thin, like it hurt to do it.

Beth touched his forehead, then called for Millie, panic already trying to climb into her voice.

William tried to smile. "Just caught something," he said. "It'll pass."

He slept in fits. Beth never really slept at all.

By morning, he was worse. His breath came shallow, like it took work to fill his lungs. His skin looked dull, and his eyes had gone too bright. Beth called Maria's mother, the midwife, because that was what folks did out here.

The midwife listened, checked him, and said it sounded like a rough flu. She told them to keep him warm, keep him drinking, give it time.

Millie watched William try to stand. His hand gripped the table, then slid, like his strength had left him.

By late afternoon, time wasn't something they had.

Millie drove. Beth sat in the passenger seat with one hand on William's knee, talking to him, begging him to stay with her. William kept trying to answer, but he had to stop between words to breathe.

The county hospital was small and bright. They put him in a bed, then another bed, then a room. People came and went. Someone said oxygen. Someone said infection. Someone said something about that mystery virus that's been going around.

Millie stood at the foot of the bed and watched machines do what lungs were supposed to do. Beth held William's hand, the last solid thing left in the room.

William turned his head toward Beth, eyes glassy, trying to focus.

"Hey," he whispered.

Beth leaned close. "I'm here."

His fingers tightened once, then loosened.

"Give our baby my buckle," he said, breath catching. "So he knows me."

Beth nodded hard, tears sliding, saying yes, yes, yes, like her voice could keep him anchored.

William opened his mouth again, like there was one more thing, something important, something only he could say.

Nothing came out.

His eyes stayed on Beth's face. Then they didn't.

The room went quiet, and it felt wrong.

Like the air itself had stepped back.

After, there was paperwork. Signatures. Questions Beth couldn't answer because her mind kept circling the same moment. Millie handled what she could. Not because she was strong, but because it had to be done.

Beth was pregnant and alone, and the ranch didn't care. The water still needed hauling. The animals still needed feed. Bills still arrived like they had a right to.

Beth learned something in those first weeks, standing in the yard with William's buckle in her palm. The ranch could survive weather, debt, even loneliness, but it couldn't fight what you couldn't see coming.

Millie took Beth in like family. Not out of duty, out of love and survival. She showed her how to hold the work without letting it swallow her. Beth showed Millie she would not run.

They hired help when they could. They did the rest themselves.

Some mornings Millie looked at Beth and saw her younger self, scared and stubborn, carrying a life into a hard country.

She put her hand on Beth's shoulder, steady and sure.

The past repeated, but softer.

And somehow, the ranch stayed standing.

CHAPTER FIFTEEN

THE SPYKER RANCH IS HIS NOW

Jake came in the spring of 1994, healthy, loud, and angry at the bright lights. Beth held him like she was scared he'd vanish if she loosened her grip. Her face was pale, her hair stuck to her temples, and her eyes kept searching the room, waiting for someone to walk in and explain how she was supposed to do this without William.

Millie didn't offer speeches. She stayed close. She handled what needed handling.

When the nurse finally laid Jake against Beth's chest, the baby's cry softened into a rough little grunt. Beth looked down, stunned, then her mouth trembled, and she kissed his forehead, holding on to him with everything she had.

Millie watched the way Beth's shoulders dropped, just a fraction, because the boy was real. He was here. The world had not taken everything.

Millie leaned in and touched two fingers to Jake's tiny fist. He grabbed her on instinct. Strong grip for someone that small. He made a sound that was half complaint, half opinion.

"Well," Millie said quietly, "you're not shy."

Beth let out a small laugh that turned into a quick wipe at her eyes. "He's loud."

"Good," Millie said. "Loud means he's breathing."

Maria showed up before the day was over, hair pinned up, sleeves rolled, carrying a bag that smelled like coffee and something warm. She took one look at Beth's face and didn't sugarcoat it.

"You're going to eat," Maria said. "Then you're going to sleep. If you don't, you'll never make it."

Beth tried to argue. Maria didn't allow it. Millie didn't either.

Back at the ranch, it became routine, the kind that saved people. Millie took nights when Beth couldn't settle. Maria took mornings when Beth needed two extra hours. Millie ran the house, stacked the bills in one place, and kept the phone calls short and clear. She didn't replace William. She didn't try. She just made sure Beth and the baby didn't get swallowed by the days.

A week later, Millie carried Jake out to the ridge at sunrise. Beth walked beside her, wrapped in a coat that didn't quite fit right anymore. Maria followed with a thermos and that look she wore when she'd already decided nobody was allowed to fall apart today.

Millie held Jake up so he could see the line of pasture, the creek bend, the fence that still needed mending. The ranch spread out in front of them, plain and honest.

"This is his," Beth whispered.

Millie kept her eyes on the land. "Not yet," she said. "For now, he borrows it. Same as we all did."

Jake squirmed and made a small noise, like he disagreed.

Millie almost smiled. "That's fine," she told him. "You'll learn. Boots first. Then work. Then you can argue."

* * *

DUST AND INHERITANCE

BETH DIDN'T TEACH Jake the ranch by pointing from the porch. She taught it the way William had learned it, the way Millie had learned it, with boots on and time spent.

When they checked fence, Beth didn't let him glance and call it done. She made him walk the line. One post at a time. Hand on the wood, fingers feeling for looseness, rot, a shift you couldn't see from ten feet away. She showed him how to listen too. Wire had its own sound, a faint hum when it was pulled too tight, a dull slack when it needed tension. Jake learned to hear it. He learned to stop rushing.

Calving season came and Beth taught him to count by pairs, not tallies. Calf to cow. Cow to calf. If you couldn't match them, you didn't really know the number. Jake carried that lesson like it mattered, because it did. A missing calf wasn't a mistake on paper, it was a problem in the pasture.

Inside, Beth kept a ledger on the kitchen table, the same spot where Millie had once stacked bills and worry. Beth didn't make it fancy. Dates, amounts, feed, vet, fuel, repairs. Jake learned to write it down straight and clean, because the ranch could forgive a lot, but it didn't forgive guesswork.

As he got older, Millie added her own lessons. She showed him how to tamp gravel around the base of a fence post with a steel bar. Slow. Steady. Not anger, not speed, just pressure and patience until the post stood solid again. Jake's hands blistered and healed, blistered and healed, and he never complained much. When he did, Maria gave him a look that ended the conversation.

They slowly became a team. Maria cooked, but Millie took turns. Beth fixed what broke and said what nobody else wanted to say. Chores were shared. Jackets got hung on the same hooks. Gloves got swapped without anyone making a big deal out of it. They wore about the same size in work clothes, so nothing fit perfect, but everything worked.

One afternoon, Millie found Clem's old shirt while sorting a box in the back room. The fabric smelled like dust and time. In the chest pocket she felt paper, folded small, worn thin from being handled.

Debt settled in full.

The words were simple. The weight behind them wasn't.

Millie sat on the edge of the bed and held the note for a long minute. She didn't cry. She just breathed. Then she folded it again, careful, and slid it into her own shirt pocket like it belonged close to her heart.

Later, Beth found it by accident when she was folding laundry. She opened it, read the line, and her face changed in a quiet way. No questions, no drama, just understanding. She refolded it the same way and put it back where she'd found it.

That shirt went into a box with old work boots and mothballs and other things nobody threw away because nobody could replace them.

Out in the yard, Millie watched Jake ride. He sat the saddle like he'd been born to it. The horse moved easy under him, the land wide and still.

The Spyker Ranch looked safe.

For now.

By the time Jake hit his mid teens, the ranch didn't look at him like a kid anymore. Folks spoke to him straight. Men at the feed store asked him questions they used to ask Beth. The banker quit saying, "Tell your grandmother," and started saying, "Tell me what you're doing."

Jake learned the job the way Millie taught everything, by doing it. He fixed what broke. He checked the water. He walked the fence when the wind came hard. He didn't pretend he knew it all, but he also didn't ask permission to carry the weight.

Millie watched him more than she spoke to him. Pride showed in small ways. An extra biscuit on his plate. A hand on his shoulder when he came in late. A quiet "Good" when he'd made the right call.

In 2011, when Jake was seventeen, Millie's body finally asked for rest.

It happened in her home, in the room she'd slept in for years. No rush of relatives, no speeches, no big scene. Maria came first, practical as ever, setting a glass of water on the nightstand, adjusting her blanket gently. Beth sat close, holding Millie's hand with both of hers, eyes swollen from trying not to cry.

Jake stood by the door at first because he didn't know where to put himself.

His grandma looked smaller than he was used to seeing her. Her hands seemed lighter, the skin thinner, the knuckles still strong. She turned her head and found him with her eyes.

"Come here," she said.

Jake moved to the bed and took her other hand. It surprised him how much grip she still had.

Millie's gaze slid past him for a moment, toward the window. Morning light lay on the floorboards. Her house felt still, as if it were listening.

"I did what I could," she said, not asking for praise, only stating it plain.

"You did more than that," Jake answered. His throat tightened, but he kept his voice level.

Millie gave him the smallest nod, like she accepted the fact and didn't need it repeated. Then she breathed in, slow, and let go. Her face didn't fight. It softened, almost relieved, like she'd been waiting for permission to stop pushing.

After she was gone, the ranch kept moving because it had to.

Less than two years later, Beth was gone too. An illness that came quick, stole her strength, and left Jake standing alone in the same yard where he'd learned to walk.

He buried her near the Ridge, in what had now become the family cemetery. He kept the ledger. He kept the fence line. He kept the house in order, because that's what Millie and Beth had taught him.

The ranch was his now.

And the quiet that followed tried hard to fill every room.

After Beth was gone, Maria didn't ask Jake what he needed. She just showed up with it.

Food came first. A pot on the stove. Bread wrapped in a towel. Coffee that stayed hot because she kept refilling the cup without making a point of it. She moved through the house as if it were partly hers, like routine mattered more than grief. Jake let her. He didn't say thank you much, but her presence and attention meant the world to him.

Maria kept him eating. She kept him sleeping in stretches longer than an hour. When he got quiet in that way that turned dangerous, she put work in front of him.

"Water's low at the east tank," she'd say. "Fence took a hit by the creek." She didn't dress it up. She didn't say she was worried. She just gave him something that had to be handled.

Years passed. Not easy ones. Just steady ones.

Jake grew into the ranch the way a man grew into boots, by wearing them until they fit. He made repairs that lasted. He kept the books clean. He learned which bills could wait a week and which ones couldn't. He stopped looking over his shoulder for someone to tell him if he was doing it right.

One late spring, Maria pulled into the yard with a cardboard box on the passenger seat. Jake met her at the truck, brow already tight, because she'd driven out without calling and that usually meant a problem.

"It's not a problem," Maria said, reading his face. "It's a dog."

She opened the box and a puppy lifted its head, ears too big for its body, eyes bright and curious. Sturdy little paws, a tail that thumped like crazy.

Jake stared. "Maria."

"Don't start," she said. "You need something that breathes and doesn't argue. Something that'll get you outside when you'd rather sit in the dark."

"I've got cattle," Jake said.

"Cattle don't sleep by your boots," Maria answered. "This one will."

The puppy climbed toward Jake like it already knew him. It sniffed his hand, licked his knuckle, then leaned in and pressed its warm weight against his palm.

Jake didn't smile. Not really. But his shoulders eased.

"What's his name?" Jake asked.

"Blue," Maria said. "Because he's going to follow you like a shadow and you'll talk to him when you won't talk to anyone else."

Jake took the puppy and held it against his chest. Blue sighed once, settled, and stayed.

That night, Jake sat on the porch with Blue curled by his boot. The air cooled. The yard went quiet. The ridge line sat out there in the dark, the same as always.

Blue lifted his head, paying sharp attention to every sound.

Jake looked toward the ridge too, not waiting for signs, not asking for comfort. Just making a choice.

Tomorrow, he'd get up. Tomorrow, he'd work. Tomorrow, he'd keep it going.

CHAPTER SIXTEEN

A PROMISE ON THE RIDGE

The good years didn't end with a crash, they ended with a grind.

Jake had put together five straight seasons where the ranch finally felt steady. Calves sold on time. Hay stacked high before first snow. Repairs handled before they turned into disasters. He even let himself buy the horse he'd wanted since he was a kid, a young black stallion with a hard eye and a big, fearless stride. He named him Spike, after his father.

Then the next season came in swinging.

Feed prices jumped. Diesel climbed. A late spring storm tore fencing down across the lower pasture, then followed it with hail that shredded the roof on the machine shed. A calf got sick, then two. The vet bill arrived with a number that made Jake stare at the paper for a long time. The tractor blew a seal. The truck started eating oil. One more thing, then one more, until "one more" became the whole week.

He cut what he could. No new equipment. No hired help. He fixed boards instead of replacing them. He skipped going to town unless it was necessary. He ate what was in the freezer and told himself it was fine. He'd been raised by people who didn't quit, and he'd learned early that the land never asked permission before it took.

But the math didn't care about pride.

By mid-summer he was behind, not ruined, just tight enough that every choice mattered. Past-due balances sat there waiting, calm and patient. Quiet trouble that didn't leave until you dealt with it.

So he went to the bank.

He told himself it was a bridge. One signature, a new note, and breathing room. The loan officer spoke in a careful voice and used words that sounded helpful: refinance, consolidate, get you through. Jake listened, nodded, and held his hat in his hands.

The papers looked clean. The terms weren't.

Past-due rolled into a fresh note, secured by the ranch. The rate reset fast. Covenants that sounded reasonable until you read the list. Requirements for cash on hand, limits on what he could sell, limits on what he could delay, limits on what counted as a bad month. Collateral language that tied everything together, land, equipment, livestock, the whole place in one knot. And a balloon later that sat there smiling, pretending it was a problem for the future.

Jake signed anyway.

He walked out telling himself he'd done the grown-up thing. He'd protected the ranch. He'd bought time.

He didn't call it what it was.

A deal that only worked if nothing went wrong.

But something always goes wrong. The next thing wasn't dramatic, it was plain. Trouble that didn't make the paper, it just emptied a man out.

A late storm came through hard and fast, then the cold held longer than it should've. Jake burned through feed he'd meant to stretch. A few calves dropped weight. One got sick, then another, and the vet came back out with that look that said, "We'll do what we can," which never meant cheap.

He didn't panic. He adjusted. He always adjusted.

But he was counting on the Millers.

The contract had sounded simple when he signed it, deliver calves in the fall window, get paid on a set price tied to market, keep the place afloat. They'd even floated a small advance early on, just enough to cover feed and buy time. Jake took it because it looked responsible, and because it kept the bank off his back for a few more weeks.

Now it was his lifeline.

And the Millers treated it that way.

First came the delays. A call that said their buyer was tied up. A text that said they needed "updated counts." Then the real words showed up, quality concerns. Weight concerns. Condition concerns. Nothing you could argue with cleanly, because it all sounded reasonable.

When Jake hauled the first load, they ran them across their scale, and the numbers came back lighter than his. They talked about shrink, about stress, about how cattle always lose some on a haul. Then they started sorting, too many on the light end, they said. Too many that would "cost them" later. They waved the contract and pointed to fine print he'd read, but never expected to feel.

Payment didn't come that week.

It didn't come the next, either.

Then the Millers started talking price. The market had shifted, they said. The contract allowed adjustments, they said. They could still honor the deal, they said, but only if Jake met them halfway. And if he didn't, they could walk.

That was when the bank called.

Mr. Davidson was friendly the first time, voice smooth, almost neighborly. Just checking in. Just making sure everything was on track. Jake told him the Millers were slow paying and that it would settle out.

Davidson didn't argue. He just got quieter.

The next call came two days later. Updated financials today. The bank needed to see them today. He used phrases Jake hated because they sounded polite while they tightened: review the exposure, protect the position.

Then came the line that mattered. If the numbers didn't improve, they'd freeze the operating line.

Jake pictured the ranch the way it looked in the early morning, posts leaning where he hadn't gotten to them yet, the old barn holding on, Spike's dark shape in the pasture, watching. It was home. It was work. It was everything.

Now it also felt like collateral.

He didn't borrow to get rich. He borrowed to survive, and survival loans always cost more than you think.

He stood on the porch after that call, looking out over the place, and realized he wasn't only fighting weather or bad luck.

He was fighting time.

Help came from the usual places first.

A neighbor offered a trailer load of hay, "just till you're back on your feet." Another told him he could float him a few head, sell now, pay later. Even the vet, on his way out, paused at the gate and said, careful and quiet, "We can work something out."

Jake thanked them. He meant it.

And he said no.

It wasn't pride for the sake of pride. Charity didn't show up as income on a bank statement. Charity didn't calm a loan covenant. Charity didn't convince Mr. Davidson that the ranch was healthy. The bank wanted clean revenue and a plan they could put in a file, then forget.

So Jake kept working, and kept thinking.

One afternoon he saddled Spike and rode the back line, checking a stretch of fence that always took longer than it should. The air was sharp, the sky clear, and the land opened out in front of him the way it always had, wide and stubborn and beautiful. Snow still sat on the far peaks. The lower pasture rolled soft and gold in the last light. The creek cut through cottonwoods that hadn't leafed yet, but you could see the green coming.

He slowed the horse and let him walk.

This place wasn't just grass and cattle. It was something people daydreamed about from offices and city sidewalks. Jake had never thought of it that way. It had always been his life, not a picture.

But it could be both.

Somebody out there would pay to be here. To work. To learn. To get their hands dirty for a week and go home with a story that sounded bigger than their regular days.

He turned Spike toward the house with the idea sitting heavy and bright in his chest.

That night he dug through old magazines on the table, the ones he'd kept out of habit. Working Ranch Magazine. The Cattleman. Ads in the back, small and plain, offering breeding stock, saddles, help wanted. He found the number, wrote it down, and stared at it until it felt less ridiculous.

Maria showed up the next morning with groceries and her usual blunt face.

"What are you looking at?" she asked, leaning over his shoulder.

He told her.

She didn't laugh. She didn't coddle him, either.

"That's not charity," she said. "That's business. The bank likes business."

He hesitated. "People won't pay for this."

Maria lifted an eyebrow. "People pay to pretend they're cowboys in a hotel. You're offering the real thing."

She helped him write the ad. Short. Clear. Honest. A working ranch, room and meals, real days, real animals, learn by doing. Limited spots. Call the number.

When Jake mailed the payment for a one-time run, he stood

at the counter a second longer than necessary. He didn't bow his head or make a show of it.

He just asked God, inside himself, to let it matter.

Then he walked out and went back to work, because that part was still his.

* * *

JAKE TOOK Blue up to the ridge on the third evening after the ads hit the magazines.

It wasn't a habit, not yet, but it was becoming one. The ridge was where he could see the whole place at once, the pastures stitched together, the barns and pens, the creek line, the house sitting steady in the middle of it all. When he was a kid, it had just been land. When he was older, it had been work. Now it felt personal. The beauty of it all was undeniable.

Blue trotted ahead, nose down, then circled back and sat close to Jake's boot. The dog's ears stayed up, taking in every sound, but he didn't wander. He stayed, as if he understood what this was.

Jake headed along the ridge toward the small family cemetery, the one that looked out over the valley. He took off his hat. He held it against his thigh a moment, then spoke, out loud, because silence wasn't helping anymore.

"Grandma," he said.

The word came out rough, then smoothed. He tried again.

"I'm trying to save what you built."

The wind moved through the grass and down into the draws. Blue's head lifted, then settled again.

Jake kept talking, slow and plain. He told her about the bank, not every detail, just enough. He told her about the Millers and their games, the delays and the pressure. Then he told her about the one thing he hadn't done yet, quit.

"I put an ad in Working Ranch Magazine," he said. "And The

Cattleman. Just one run. Folks come here, they work, they learn, they get room and meals. They pay for the week or more. I get labor I can't afford, and income the bank can't ignore."

Blue shifted closer, his shoulder against Jake's boot.

Jake looked down at the dog, then out at the ranch again. "It's not charity. It's a real plan."

He let that sit in the air, then turned his eyes toward the house. The porch light was on. It made a small warm square in the dusk.

"Ma," he said, voice lower.

He didn't need her out here to hear it. He needed to say it.

"I won't let you down. I won't let this place go."

His throat tightened, but he didn't stop. He'd spent too many years swallowing promises and calling it strength. This one had to be said. This one had to be felt.

He put his hat back on and started down the ridge with Blue at his side. The ranch stretched around them, quiet, waiting, the same as it had always been. But Jake wasn't waiting anymore.

He had a plan. He had motion. He had something that wasn't fear.

Two days later, the phone rang while he was mending a gate.

He glanced at the screen, expecting Davidson, expecting another tight voice and another deadline.

Instead, the number wasn't Montana.

Jake answered, and listened, and his mouth pulled into a smile he didn't have to force.

"Yes," he said, looking out over the pasture where Spike stood black against the grass. "That's me. You're calling about the ad."

He listened again, then nodded once.

"Yeah," he said. "I've got room."

He hung up a minute later with a date on the calendar and a little air in his chest again.

EPILOGUE

HOPE, NOT LOST

The notification hit his phone as a mistake.

Jake had been standing at the kitchen counter, one boot hooked on the rung of a chair, sorting mail into two piles. The first pile was the kind you could breathe around, feed store flyer, church bulletin, a postcard from a cousin who liked mountains but didn't like work. The second pile was the one that sat heavier than paper ever should, bank envelope, insurance statement, county notice, all of it printed in that polite ink that never apologized.

He didn't open the bank envelope right away. Not because he was scared of it, he'd gotten used to fear living in the house. He was tired of letting paper tell him what kind of man he was.

Blue sat a few feet away, watching him. Not begging. Not pacing. Just there, the way that dog always was when Jake's thoughts got too loud. His ears twitched once, as though he'd heard something outside, then he settled again, chin on his paws.

Jake flipped the last envelope over, looking for anything that wasn't a bill.

That was when his phone buzzed.

A short vibration. One ping. Then a second.

He pulled it from his pocket, thumb already braced for another reminder he didn't need. Past due. Auto draft. Low balance.

Instead, the screen read:

Deposit received.

He stared at it, the words not quite fitting.

For a second he thought it had to be a refund. Some kind of reversal. A system error that would straighten itself out, then slap him with a fee for existing.

He tapped it open.

The amount wasn't life changing. It wasn't "ranch saved" money. But it was real, and it was in the black, and it was sitting in his account where it belonged.

Jake's throat tightened, then loosened again. He read the name attached to it.

Contadelucci.

He blinked once. Then again.

He'd seen plenty of names come through the ranch over the years, locals, cousins, the occasional tourist who wanted to pet a horse and call it "real life." But this one hit different. Too many syllables. Too smooth. It came from a world where people didn't patch fences with baling wire and prayer.

He glanced at Blue, as if the dog might have an opinion on Italian last names.

Blue didn't move. He just looked back with that steady, calm stare, the one that always seemed to say: *Well? What are we doing?*

Jake set the phone on the counter and opened his laptop. The old thing took its time, as if it had to consider whether this was worth waking up for. The screen lit, the ranch Wi-Fi hiccuped, then caught.

He logged into the account. Checked it twice. Then a third time because hope made him suspicious.

Still there.

Still real.

The deposit matched the "ranch experience program" setup he'd almost talked himself out of finishing. The one Tommy had pushed, half joking, half serious. The one Maria had called "a fancy word for letting people pay to watch you work."

Jake had built a simple ad. Nothing polished. Just honest. A little history, a short list of chores, a promise of early mornings, real meals, and work that meant something.

He'd written it in plain language because he didn't know how to sell something he'd been born into. He'd only known how to keep it alive.

Then he'd told himself he hadn't done it for money, he'd done it for options.

Options were a nice word for desperation, but he could live with it.

He clicked the reservation details.

Three months. One guest. The deposit covered the first month, real money, real commitment. Someone had read his words and trusted the ranch enough to stake a season on it.

He sat down slowly at the table, not because his legs gave out, but because he didn't trust the moment not to vanish if he moved too fast. His hands rested on the wood, the same table that had held so many quiet battles, budgets scribbled on scrap paper, repair lists, cold coffee, grief that never left a stain but never really cleaned up either.

The house was quiet. Too quiet.

That quiet had been Ma's, once. Quiet in the way she moved through rooms after Dad died, as though sound might break something that was barely holding.

Then it had been Grandma's. Quiet in the way she sat on the porch some evenings, eyes on the ridge, hands folded as if she was keeping herself in one piece by force of will. Jake had been young then, old enough to feel the shape of loss, too young to name it cleanly.

Grandma didn't talk about the past the way most people did. She didn't romanticize it. She didn't soften it. She'd tell a story the way you drove fence posts, straight down, no wobble.

But Jake had learned anyway. From watching. From the way she checked the pump first thing in the morning, water still a miracle worth confirming. From how she handled paper, not with trust, but with readiness.

From how she never acted as though the ranch was guaranteed.

It wasn't.

That was the whole point.

Jake lifted the phone again. He stared at the number attached to the reservation, then set it down without calling. Not yet. The program's confirmation message would handle the basics. He didn't need to talk himself into sounding foolish with a stranger on the other end.

Still, he couldn't stop looking at the name.

Contadelucci.

He said it once under his breath, testing it.

It sounded like money and trouble wrapped up in the same package. Mostly, it sounded like a person used to being listened to.

And it sounded like the beginning of something.

He opened the reservation again and read the notes field, half expecting it to be blank. It wasn't. Just one line, polite and confident. Looking forward to learning. Please confirm directions to the ranch house.

Jake stared at it a moment, then nodded to himself. He wasn't ready for the whole future, but he could handle directions. He could handle a welcome. He could handle one person showing up and seeing the place the way it really was.

Blue stood and stretched, then walked to the back door. He paused there and looked over his shoulder, waiting.

Jake understood.

"Yeah," he murmured. "I know."

He grabbed his jacket and followed Blue outside.

The air had a bite to it. Not the deep winter kind, but the kind that reminded you Montana didn't care how hard your day had been.

Blue trotted ahead, not running, not dawdling. Purposeful. It felt like a patrol, as if it mattered to check the land even when the land wasn't asking.

Jake mounted Spike and rode up toward the ridge. He could smell dry grass, old wood, the faint clean bite of cold.

Halfway up, he stopped.

From there, he could see the ranch the way Millie used to look at it, not as property, not as an investment, but as work that had to be done again tomorrow.

The creek line cut through the pasture. The cottonwoods stood along it as sentries. Farther out, the fence line glinted. The world looked calm, but Jake knew better. The world always looked calm right before it asked you to prove you deserved it.

Blue trotted close to Spike's left side, steady as a shadow, eyes scanning as if the whole valley belonged to his watch.

Jake took a long breath in. Held it. Let it out slow.

He felt something shift inside him, not fixed, not healed, just loosened.

It wasn't joy, at least not the loud kind. It was steadier, settling in his chest like the first deep breath after a long run. Relief. Maybe even possibility.

He thought about his father. William "Spike" Spyker, the name on the headstone that never got old no matter how many years passed. He'd never known him, not really, but he'd spent his whole life walking through the echo of him. In the way the men in town would look at Jake and see someone else for a split second. In the way Maria would sometimes say, "You've got his hands," as if that explained anything.

He thought about his Ma. About the quiet strength she'd carried until it wore her down. About the way she had loved this place and still lost pieces of herself to it.

Then his Grandma. The backbone of it all. The woman who had taken a hard piece of land and refused to let it win. The woman who had built a life on dust and stubbornness, and whatever faith looked like when you were too tired to make it pretty.

Jake whispered, low enough that only Blue and the ridge heard it.

"We got one."

Blue's ear flicked.

Jake huffed a short laugh, almost embarrassed by himself. "Not a miracle. Just… one."

He pulled the phone from his pocket again. The screen was dim now, but the deposit notice still sat there, bright and impossible.

A guest.

A deposit.

A name that didn't belong in his world, and yet, somehow, had reached into it.

He stared out over the ranch again and tried to picture what "tomorrow" looked like. Not as a threat. Not as a bill. Not as a countdown.

Just a day.

Just work.

Just one more chance to hold the line.

He put the phone away and rested his hands on his hips, shoulders rolling back as if he was shaking off a weight he'd been carrying too long.

Blue stood up and nudged his knee once, gentle but insistent.

"Alright," Jake said. "Let's go home."

Jake rode Spike back down. Blue right next to them. The

porch light small and steady in the dark. The house waited with its creaks and its memories and its worn corners that still felt like family. The ranch sat quiet beyond it, not asking for promises, only effort.

At the door, Jake paused and looked back one last time.

The ranch wasn't saved yet, but it wasn't lost either, and that was something.

THE INSPIRATION

Fiction borrows from reality, but sometimes reality beats fiction to the punch. The Clem and Millie you met in these pages were born from the real Clem and Millie Spyker, pictured above.

While the plot of this book is a story I spun, the grit, the stubbornness, and the way they stood beside each other when the world got heavy, that part is all true. They built a life not on easy promises, but on the kind of work that doesn't ask for applause. This book is my way of keeping their names, and their fire, alive.

ABOUT THE AUTHOR

Kirk Voclain writes stories about grit, heart, and the trouble we get into when we follow both. He believes books should move fast, feel true, and leave you a little lighter when you turn the last page. South Louisiana is home. That rhythm shows up in his voice. So do porch conversations, strong coffee, and people who keep their promises.

By day, Kirk does for a living what most call a hobby. By night, he does for a hobby what most call a profession. Photography pays the bills. Writing feeds the fire. He is happiest when the scene on the page clicks into focus and the characters refuse to stand still.

His debut thriller, **Double Exposure**, introduced readers to high stakes and a hero who never blinks. With **Dust and Inheritance**, he takes readers back to the beginning of the Spyker legacy, setting the stage for the modern-day struggles and romance found in his novel **Boots and Stilettos**. More novels are in the works… because of course they are.

Kirk also runs Pro4uM.com, a long-running creative community where working pros swap ideas, sharpen skills, and say the quiet parts out loud. Teaching and encouraging others is part of his DNA.

That same drive to help creators led him to launch FiiP.net (Fresh Indie Ink Promotions). FiiP is a platform built for authors who are tired of shouting into the void. It's about real visibility, honest contests, and helping indie voices find the readers they deserve. No fake hype, just fresh ink and the spotlight it earns.

For news, extras, and contact info, visit kirkvoclain.com. If you enjoyed this book, a short review helps more than you know. Thank you for reading... truly.

Connect with him personally on any of his social accounts.

- instagram.com/kirkvoclain
- facebook.com/kirk.voclain
- tiktok.com/@kirkvoclain
- linkedin.com/in/kirkvoclain
- x.com/kirkvoclain
- youtube.com/kirkvoclain
- amazon.com/stores/author/B0FWB8H5VL
- goodreads.com/kirkvoclain

ALSO BY KIRK VOCLAIN

Double Exposure

Code In The Grain

Read the sequel here next: Boots and Stilettos

And more to come! Join our mailing list to be notified of future releases: https://kirkvoclain.com

BOOTS AND STILETTOS

SEQUEL TO DUST AND INHERITANCE

PROLOGUE

THE PLANE TICKET

She almost didn't board the plane.

Her boarding pass sat there on the gate counter, mocking her. Row 12C, economy, no champagne, no silk pillow, no carefully curated playlist of Italian opera.

Just a one-way ticket to Montana.

Montana.

An entire state that sounded like it had more cows than people and absolutely no concept of designer anything.

Antoinette Contadelucci, heiress to one of Europe's most luxurious fashion empires, stood alone at Gate 28, now with a boarding pass in one hand and a thousand doubts in the other.

This wasn't a vacation. It wasn't a business trip. This was exile. Sent to "learn the family business," her father said. Sent to "grow up," Ricardo had sneered.

But deep down, if she was honest, she'd bought this ticket herself. Not with money. With pride. With stubbornness. With something that ached just beneath her ribs, something she couldn't quite name.

The gate agent called final boarding.

Antoinette took a breath. She looked at her reflection in the airport window. Mascara flawless. Lipstick sharp. But her eyes…

They didn't look ready.

Still, she walked forward.

She didn't know she was stepping off that plane into dirt roads and disaster, or that the man waiting at the gate would look at her like she was a puzzle he didn't want to solve. She boarded anyway.

CHAPTER ONE

BIG SKY COLLISION

The sun dipped low over the Montana plains, casting a golden glow across the rugged land. Jake Spyker leaned against the weathered post of the corral, his hat tipped back just enough to reveal blue eyes as dark as the black coffee he started his day with. The evening breeze carried the familiar scents of sage and prairie grass, mixed with the earthier notes of cattle and leather from the nearby barn. He was wiry, the kind of skinny that comes from years of hard work under the sun, with a quiet strength hidden beneath the dust on his shirt. Life out here didn't leave room for much more than cattle and long stretches of silence, broken only by the occasional lowing of cattle or cry of a hawk riding the thermals above. That was fine by him... until she showed up.

Antoinette Contadelucci stepped out of the truck like a dream misplaced, the setting sun catching her arrival like nature's own spotlight. Her golden hair caught the breeze, tumbling in waves over her shoulders, and her every movement carried the effortless grace of her Italian roots. The contrast between her and the rustic ranch setting was almost jarring, like finding a pearl in a feed bucket. Jake had seen her kind before, at least, he thought he had. The tourists who came through Montana every summer looking for adventure, snapping photos of wide-open spaces before retreating to their big city lives, leaving nothing behind but tire tracks and forgotten coffee cups from the local diner. But there was something different about Antoinette, or Annie, as she preferred to be called. She wasn't a tourist. She was here for something more, and that something glinted in her eyes like steel beneath silk.

She walked toward him, her heels crunching on the gravel with each deliberate step, a sharp contrast to the soft melody of her accent when she said, "You must be Jake? Or do you prefer Jacob?" She met his gaze with eyes as blue as the big Montana sky. Her words were warm, yet he sensed a spark of challenge, as if she'd already decided she wasn't impressed by the man in dusty boots, wearing his dad's old belt buckle stamped with "SPIKE."

Jake straightened and tipped his hat in greeting, feeling the familiar weight of responsibility that came with the ranch pressing down on his shoulders. He knew why she was here. It had all been arranged by her father, Dante. Emails, phone calls, payments, arrangements, everything had been set weeks ago. Jake didn't know why his ranch had been chosen, only that he needed the money they were willing to pay. Whatever had brought her to this exact stretch of nowhere, he couldn't say, but he had a feeling she was about to turn his world upside down.

"Jake's fine," he said, his voice rough from disuse. The ranch didn't offer much opportunity for conversation beyond the occasional grunt at the feed store or quick words with the veterinarian. Even the weekly supply runs into town had become exercises in efficiency rather than social calls. He studied her carefully, noting the designer label on her jacket that probably cost more than his monthly feed bill. The jacket was beautiful, he had to admit, but about as practical for ranch work as snow shoes in July. "Your father called ahead. Said you needed to learn about ranch operations."

Annie's perfectly shaped eyebrows arched slightly, a gesture that managed to be both elegant and slightly defensive. "Ah, so you know why I'm here. Did he tell you everything?" There was something in her tone that suggested layers of meaning, stories untold, and Jake found himself curious despite his better judgment.

"Just that you're taking over the family's agricultural investment division, and he wants you to understand the business from the ground up." Jake pushed away from the post, gesturing toward the sprawling ranch behind him, where the evening light painted the pastures in shades of gold and amber. A small herd of cattle grazed in the distance, their shapes dark against the sunset. "Though I got to say, seems like an awful long way to come from Milan just to look at some cows."

A flash of irritation crossed her face, like lightning in clear skies. "Milano," she corrected automatically, then caught herself and smiled, transforming her face from merely beautiful to something that made Jake's chest tight. "And there's more to it than just looking at cows, Mr. Spyker. My father may see this as just another investment, but I..." She paused, looking out across the vast expanse of land, something vulnerable flickering across her features. The wind caught her hair again, and for a moment she looked less like an Italian heiress and more like someone searching for solid ground. "I need to prove something."

The wind picked up, and Jake watched as Annie pulled her jacket closer, her citified perfume mixing with the earthy smells of the ranch. She wasn't dressed for what was coming, neither the weather nor the work ahead. Her delicate shoes already showed signs of defeat from the rough ranch ground.

"Storm's rolling in," he said, nodding toward the darkening western sky, where clouds were building like a mountain range of their own. "Best get you settled in the guest house before it hits. We can start your... education tomorrow morning. Five AM sharp."

Annie's eyes widened slightly, feeling the full weight of the distance and time zones she had just traveled. She wasn't sure she heard him correctly. "Five? In the morning?"

"Cattle don't care much for sleeping in," Jake replied, the ghost of a smile tugging at his lips. A nearby horse nickered softly, as if agreeing. "And if you're serious about learning this business, you'll need to see it all, including the parts that don't make it into your father's quarterly reports."

Secretly wishing she could have just one day to settle in, she lifted her chin, meeting his gaze with a determination that seemed to come from somewhere deeper than her polished exterior. "I'll be ready."

Jake doubted that, but he kept the thought to himself. Instead, he watched as she turned back to her truck, presumably to gather her things. Her confident stride faltered slightly as her heel sunk into a patch of soft earth, and he found himself moving forward instinctively to steady her, his rancher's instincts overriding his intention to maintain distance. His hand caught her elbow, and for a brief moment, they were close enough for him to see the flecks of gold in her blue eyes and smell her soft floral perfume.

"Careful," he murmured, quickly stepping back, trying to ignore the warmth that lingered on his palm. "Ground can be treacherous out here."

"I'm beginning to see that," Annie replied softly, and Jake had the distinct impression she wasn't just talking about the dirt beneath her feet. Something passed between them then, quick as a shadow from a passing cloud, but just as real.

Thunder rumbled in the distance as Jake helped her with her luggage, three expensive-looking suitcases that seemed better suited for a European fashion week than a working ranch. The leather was butter-soft, the hardware gleaming gold, and he tried not to think about how they'd look after a few weeks of ranch dust. The guest house was simple but clean, with a small covered porch and windows that looked out over the western pasture. It had been his grandmother's house once, before she passed, and something about seeing this polished city woman ascending those worn wooden steps made his chest tight with an emotion he couldn't quite name.

"It's... rustic," Annie said, taking in the modest accommodations. But there was no judgment in her voice, only curiosity, and perhaps a touch of appreciation for the way the setting sun painted the weathered wood in shades of honey and gold. A hummingbird darted past, checking out the feeder his grandmother had hung years ago, and Annie's face lit up at the sight.

"It's home," Jake replied simply, watching her reaction to the tiny bird. "Or it will be, for the next few months at least." He set her bags inside the door and stepped back onto the porch, breathing in the storm-heavy air. "There's coffee and basic supplies in the kitchen. Bathroom's down the hall. If you need anything else, my house is just over that rise." He pointed to the slightly larger structure about a quarter-mile away, where smoke curled from the chimney despite the warm evening.

Annie followed his gesture, then turned back to him with an unreadable expression. "You live alone?"

"Just me and Blue," he answered, referring to his aging cattle dog who was probably already curled up by the fireplace, keeping watch over the ranch in his own way. "And Spike," he added, a slight smile touching his lips as he thought of the stubborn black stallion he'd named after his father. The horse had been his faithful partner through every cattle drive and midnight emergency for the past decade. The horse was more friend than livestock, with a personality as big as the Montana sky. "And about three hundred head of cattle, give or take."

He hesitated, then added, "I couldn't do it without Maria. She lives next door. She cooks more than I ask her to."

Annie tilted her head. "You have a cook?"

"She'd laugh if she heard you say that," Jake said. "She's been around since my mom was alive. Decided somewhere along the way that I'd starve without her." He shrugged. "Her husband Carlos doesn't mind, and she hardly charges me. Closest thing to family out here, I guess. After Blue."

"No wife? No family?" The question seemed to surprise her as much as it did him, and she quickly added, "I'm sorry, that's none of my business." A blush colored her cheeks, making her look younger, more vulnerable.

Jake adjusted his hat, buying time before responding, feeling the worn leather band that had molded to his head over countless days under the Montana sun. "No ma'am. Never found anyone who loved this land as much as I do." The words came out more honest than he'd intended, carrying the weight of lonely nights and quiet mornings, and he cleared his throat awkwardly. "But I guess Maria, and Tommy who helps out around here, would qualify as family. Anyway, I'll leave you to get settled. Remember, five AM."

"I won't forget," she said, and there was that challenge in her eyes again, mixed with something softer that made him want to linger on the porch longer than he should. The first stars were beginning to appear in the eastern sky, and for a moment, they were reflected in her eyes.

The first fat drops of rain began to fall as Jake made his way back to his own house, his boots leaving deep prints in the increasingly muddy ground. Behind him, lights began to glow in the windows of the guest house, warm and inviting against the gathering storm. He tried not to think about how those lights would shine across the pasture every evening now, or how they might make the ranch feel a little less empty.

Blue greeted him at the door with a questioning look, as if to ask what he made of their new guest. Jake scratched behind the dog's ears, considering the same question himself. Annie Contadelucci was clearly out of her element here, armed with designer clothes and big city expectations. She'd probably last a week, maybe two, before running back to her comfortable life in Italy. And yet...

And yet there had been something in her eyes when she looked out across the ranch, something that reminded him of the way he'd felt the first time he'd seen this land. Like she was searching for something she couldn't quite name, something that might just be hidden in the vast spaces between earth and sky.

Thunder cracked overhead, and Blue pressed closer to his leg, his warm presence a comfort against the growing storm. Jake moved to the window, watching as rain swept across the plains in silvery sheets, transforming the dusty ranch into something wild and mysterious. The lights in the guest house remained steady and bright, a beacon in the gathering darkness, like a promise or a warning, he wasn't sure which. Whatever Annie was looking for, whatever she needed to prove, to her father or to herself, Jake had a feeling the next few months were going to change them both in ways neither of them could predict.

He just hoped his heart was ready for the storm that was coming.

www.ingramcontent.com/pod-product-compliance
Lightning Source LLC
LaVergne TN
LVHW010210070526
838199LV00062B/4521